SNOW GLOBE TRAVELER

a novel

V.M. BRENDEL

ISBN 979-8-9900762-0-4

For Ray who believed in me and encouraged me to continue telling Jade's story.

Chapter One

Spring Creek 2011

SULLY'S FRIENDS, EVERY ONE OF THEM SHOWED UP. Pete, Roberto, Jimmy, and Omar surrounded and comforted me, yet I was alone in a crowded room. They assured me they would be there for me, but they were Sully's friends, not mine.

The memorial service was prolonged by the numerous stories so many needed to tell. Mechanically, I traveled through the motions, pretended to listen to their stories, received too many hugs along with the obligatory sympathetic head tilt, and then thanked them for their condolences. Imagining life without Sully invaded my every thought—a life without the father I'd only met a few years ago.

Finally, in the solace of my apartment, I released my grief into the silence. It was as if my apartment had been lined with acoustic panels which absorbed my sobs resulting in an eerily tranquil room. The lump that had wedged in my throat resisted my continuous attempt to swallow it away. It was also impervious to the eight ounces of water and was even immune to a shot of whiskey—a last exasperated effort. I hugged Sully's urn and talked to him as if he were sitting next to me. "I need you," I whispered. And then I yelled, "How could you leave me?"

I had an urge to hurl his urn across the room but knew I would immediately regret it. So, before I acted on that urge, I placed it on the table next to the piece of pottery he had made for me. *Love has betrayed me once again.*

I spent the rest of the evening and several hours past midnight with a mixture of pacing and crying. Around two a.m. I'd cried so hard that what little food I'd had that day refused to stay down. I sipped some ginger ale to settle my stomach, but it did not settle my nerves.

Sometime after that, I finally drifted off to sleep. However, around four a.m. Sully's parents called to see how the service went. I guessed they'd forgotten about the time difference. They wanted to make sure I knew how sorry they were that they couldn't be there for me. It was a bit awkward since I had never met them in person and in the past, Sully had usually carried the conversations. They didn't think they could endure the long flight from London but promised that as soon as they were in better health, they would come visit me in the United States.

I hadn't predicted how emotionally draining a memorial service would be. Sully had emphatically spelled out in his will that he did not want a viewing and had requested only a small service. It turned out to be anything but small. Since I'd had months to accept his death, I thought I'd be able to return to work the next day. But it was more difficult than I had imagined, and I regretted not requesting the day off after the memorial service. I was already on thin ice with Mr. Avery, one of the attorneys, so I knew it wasn't wise to call off at the last minute.

I could barely lift my head off my pillow, and my arms felt as if I was carrying ten-pound weights in each hand. My body ached deep into the marrow of my bones. I summoned what little strength I had and dragged myself into the shower hoping it would wake me. It helped somewhat, but I knew in order to make it through the day, I'd need mega doses of caffeine.

On my way to work, I stopped at the Coffee Coffee Coffee House for overpriced java to keep my eyelids propped open and to fulfill my caffeine addiction. The line inside extended almost to the doorway. Seemed I wasn't the only one who had an insatiable need for a morning jolt. I was certain not one person in line needed the caffeine as much as I had. It was probably just part of their typical morning routines. Except the lady with a toddler and an infant in tow, she appeared frazzled. I assumed that she'd probably had less sleep than I had. The toddler attached herself to her mom's leg as if her arms were strips of Velcro. I winked at her, and she momentarily peeled one arm off and opened and closed her pudgy fingers to reply with a toddler wave. *I thought I'd have been a mom or at least had an option to have been starting a family by the time I was thirty.* Nicholas had shattered that dream. Why can't adults be more like kids—honest, trustworthy, and innocent?

Finally, there was only one more person ahead of me, which should have ensured I would not be late for work. However, as past experiences reminded me, I'm a magnet for bad luck. And sure enough, the lady in front of me seemed to be ordering for her entire office staff. I would most likely be late but was unwilling to give up. Of course, when it was my turn the barista decided it was time to refill the container of wooden stirrers even though it was not entirely empty. I was certainly going to be late. However, at that point I was more than committed to the challenge. I plopped my purse onto the counter and forced a loud lengthy sigh to get her attention which did not seem to produce the outcome I needed. I retrieved my phone from the outside pocket of my bag to check the time just as my purse toppled to the floor scattering most of the contents. While on my knees gathering my belongings, I heard, "Next."

I placed my order from a kneeling position on the floor. Finally, my perseverance propelled me to victory. My prize, a tall cup of caffeine and two packets of raw sugar.

Purse slung over my shoulder and coffee in hand, I sprinted toward the door. However, the calm morning had shifted quite abruptly. Outside the coffee house, abandoned plastic shopping bags whisked by like whirling dervishes. Their flights reminded me of spinning laundry in rows of clothes dryers at the laundromat. White and blue t-shirt-like bags tumbled up and down and left to right.

I had heard the forecast that morning, but I clearly must have been daydreaming. Listening but not paying attention. I could swear Ronald Dante on Channel Two News had said there was a slight possibility of rain, but the temperature was to be normal.

Looking at the dark ominous sky, the slight possibility had turned imminent. Was this how Dorothy felt as she attempted to return to the safety of the farm? Ronald must have missed the memo that in Spring Creek "normal" at that time of year was usually in the mid to upper seventies, not sixty with a windchill which made it feel like thirty. His forecast was why I had made the decision to leave my umbrella and coat at home. I supposed they were keeping my closet safe, dry, and warm. A better choice may have been to have used the weather app on my phone instead of listening to old Ronnie. Oh, to have a job where I would have a six-digit salary and could still be incorrect most of the time.

Clutching my coffee as though it were a revered security blanket, I headed toward my destination, but only made it to the next block. Grateful to still be dry, I huddled under the awning of the Weary Traveler's Antique Treasures as a torrential downpour erupted. It then quickly turned into what can only be described as Armageddon. The wind whipped at the striped awning flapping the scallops like birds in flight. My white silk blouse, a recent splurge for my thirtieth birthday, would be ruined if I attempted to go on. Surprised but grateful that the shop under whose awning I took refuge appeared to be open even this early. So, I ducked inside.

5

"Welcome!" sang a booming voice.

I had obviously heard her but could not locate the person belonging to the sing-songy welcome. "Hello?" I replied, directed toward the point from where I assumed the voice had come.

A woman popped up from behind the ornately carved wooden counter like bread in an overactive toaster. She sported a head full of artificially colored bright red spikey hair which sprang out in various directions like a mass of corkscrews.

"Are you open?" I glanced around to see if there were any other customers. "The door was unlocked. I hope it was okay that I came in."

"I'm open if you need me to be." Her lips extended from one ear to the other, seeming to take up the bottom third of her face, and they were painted with bright red lipstick duplicating her hair color. Her smile revealed a smudge of the same red on her two very white front teeth. "It's so nice of you to join us."

I glanced around the store again looking for the other part of *us*. I must have heard her incorrectly as I seemed to be the only other person there.

"I was on my way to work and got caught in this downpour and—"

She interrupted, "Isn't this rain grand? Like giving the earth a nice refreshing drink. I just love it. Don't you? It's the heavens blessing us with sustenance."

Crack. A bolt of lightning lit up the sky and shook the large front windows. After the temporary fireworks display, it looked as if a dark curtain had been placed over the windows. The storm had thrust the early morning hour into an unnatural darkness and tricked the streetlights into automatically turning on as if it were nearly nightfall.

The wild-haired lady chattered on about her love for rain. I grimaced a smile. *Seems she's quite an optimist.* As she rattled on, I pictured her sentences as devoid of any punctuation—no commas, no semicolons, and no periods. Her endless stream of words seemed to develop into continuous run-on sentences.

I was not in the mood for pleasantries as my thoughts were focused on how I was going to manage to get to work dry and not too terribly late. However, like most things in my life, the circumstances seemed to be out of my control.

"I'm Zelda, darling. And welcome to my little slice of heaven."

I wonder if "darling" is part of her name or if she is addressing me as darling.

Her left arm was festooned with shiny metal bangle bracelets that clanged when she threw her arm toward me as if she were throwing a baseball, apparently to shake my hand. I felt an unwarranted desire to duck from the invisible baseball, but instead, I cautiously approached the counter and awkwardly shook her outstretched hand. Her short nails were painted a fiery red - a similar hue to her lips and hair color.

"I'm Jade. Jade Fair." My eyes crinkled in unfair judgment. I hated when people judged me. *Stop it, Jade. Stop judging this woman. You don't even know her or her story.*

"Well, pleased to meet you, Jade, Jade Fair very pleased indeed and what a fine name, Jade Fair. Such a fine name which suits you very well, very well indeed."

"Thank you."

"I'm guessing you were blessed with the name Jade because of those lovely green eyes. They are strikingly mesmerizing. I would be amiss if I didn't say that they are much more beautiful than the actual stone."

"Jade was my mother's favorite gemstone, and she had told me that in some cultures, it's a symbol of heaven."

"Hmmm. Heaven. Heaven. Yes. A wise and spiritual woman, your mother!" Zelda nodded.

I masked my discomfort with a smile. I did not want to get into the dysfunctional relationship between my mother and me.

"And what can we help you with today, Miss Jade Fair with the heavenly eyes?" Still holding my left hand from the handshake, she glanced at my ringless finger confident I was a Miss, and she was quite correct. I gazed at the naked finger that just three years ago had been adorned with a two-carat princess cut diamond. I awkwardly attempted to pull my hand from her embrace. Probably sensing my uneasiness, she smiled and patted my hand gently placing it onto the counter. Zelda then bounced out from behind her perch and locked her arm in mine as if we were best friends ready to take a stroll in the park.

"As I mentioned, I was on my way to work and got caught in—"

"Yes. I recall. But surely there is something that interests you in our vast display of treasures." She swiped her arms across the room and back as if she was a prima ballerina. "As you can see, we have lovely tables, chairs, settees, armoires, clocks, jewelry, and so, so, so much more. I'm certain we have something that will suit your fancy or perhaps you have a question or two or maybe even three that you are just burning to ask us?"

I don't think she took a breath through that entire soliloquy.

The rain had not let up, and I felt uncomfortable just standing there with only the intention of keeping myself and my blouse dry. I felt cornered into answering her. So, I scoured the store for something to use in conversation. Next to me was a round antique side table with glass ball-and-claw legs. On top of the table was a hand-crocheted ivory lace tablecloth with what appeared to be a tea or coffee stain in its middle. Nice, but not my taste—the table nor the lace. Besides, I didn't have a lot of room in my tiny apartment for any more furniture, and antiques reminded me of my stuffy grandmother's house which was never very welcoming.

Tchotchkes just end up being dust collectors, and I was not the tidiest housekeeper, so that was a definite capital N, capital O.

Zelda must have noticed I had scrutinized the rather large stain. She stealthily moved toward it in a kind of ballet move and placed a large blue and white vase over the unwanted markings. She almost had me believing I had not seen the spot.

"Are you a collector?" she asked. "Perhaps a collector of teacups, or dolls, or swords."

I shook my head.

"Here is a fine collection of rare antique maps." She placed one hand on my shoulder and pointed toward the framed maps with her other arm as if she was a sailor pointing toward land. She nudged me closer to the maps which hung on the wall above a dining table. I had no interest in displaying on my apartment walls anything that might remind me, no taunt me, that I had never traveled outside of the United States. Sadly, I'd actually only been to a number of states fewer than the fingers on one hand.

To appease this woman, I searched for some conversation piece. I finally spied a rather large collection of snow globes that looked quite eclectic. There were at least ten on top of an antique dresser, another twenty or so on a mid-century style kitchen table, and too many to count on the shelves of a wooden barrister bookcase. "How did you come to have so many snow globes?" I asked.

"An auction. Didn't you notice we were closed one day last week so I could travel to Embersville? I had a feeling it was going to be a great one. And my senses did not disappoint."

"You had to close? But I thought you'd said 'we.' Couldn't your partner have kept the store open?"

"My dear! I own and run this shop entirely by myself." She closed her eyes and smiled. "These treasures are my precious friends. So, I always include them as my partners. We are in business together." She opened her eyes and tossed a quick wink my way.

I glanced toward the windows to see if the shroud had lifted. It had not. I wanted nothing more than to exit as soon as possible in order to avoid being extremely late for work. *Crack.* Another bolt of lightning again shook the large front windows. Wacky weather day. Wacky shop owner.

"You admire our snow globe collection, yes?"

"They're lovely." I was not just being polite. They really were quite lovely.

"The story told to me was that this is only part of a collection which was owned by a nearly one-hundred-year-old woman."

"You mean one person owned all of these?" A picture of a very old woman with snow globes piled all around her instantly popped into my head and I couldn't help but chuckle. I'd heard of crazy cat ladies but never crazy snow globe ladies.

11

"It really is quite a touching story." Zelda raised one eyebrow. "I believe her father was in the military, or he was a diplomat or something like that. Anyway, they had a very special bond and when he had traveled or when they had traveled together, he would purchase snow globes for her. That really doesn't matter. What does matter though, is that when he died, she had continued the tradition, probably in honor of her father."

What tradition could I possibly continue to honor Sully? All I have from him is his professional chef's knife set and I'm certainly not going to start a culinary knife collection. A new image of a woman surrounded by a knife collection interrupted my thoughts. I bit my lip to suppress a chuckle anxious to escape.

I ran my hand over the snow globe's glass of the one from Italy. It had a model of the Pisa Tower in the middle of the globe. The feel of the glass reminded me of the bosc pears Sully would have me feel for ripeness. He'd used the cold hard flesh of the pears in his roasted brussels sprouts recipe. My mouth watered just thinking about it.

"Can I interest you in purchasing one, or two, darling?" Zelda held up one of the larger ones. She turned it from side to side. The fake snow twirled and drifted around what appeared to be a cathedral or perhaps a palace.

"They are lovely, but I've no room for knickknacks in my tiny apartment." I shrugged.

Zelda sighed. "My motto has always been: 'Make room for beautiful things, for they hold in them the power to encourage your hopes and dreams.' No?" She again directed a warm smile and wink toward me.

Hopes. Dreams. Hah. What a joke. My dreams had faded into oblivion the moment I had learned my entire life was a sham perpetuated by my mother's lies. And my hopes dissipated when the series of strokes cemented Sully's battle with life.

"What are your hopes and dreams, darling?" Zelda rescued me from my miserable thoughts. She had an accent I couldn't quite place. But whether her sentences were questions or not, she ended each one of them with a higher pitch than she had begun and included a quick wink. During our short chat, I felt genuinely warmed by her smile and especially her wink, which softened my initial judgement of her thus convincing me that I was indeed special in her evaluation.

"Besides, these are enchanting. Don't you think?" Zelda took my take-out coffee cup, set it on a nearby table, and placed into my hands a globe with the word Vienna on its base. As if she didn't trust me, she cupped her hands below mine like I was a child incapable of independently handling the object.

Zelda did not wait for my response. She continued, "Did you know the first snow globe was of the Mariazell Basilica in Mariazell, Austria?"

"I guess I've never wondered much about snow globes." I glided the globe back and forth with both hands clasped around the glass to show her I was indeed capable of keeping it safe. The snow floated down upon the miniature building. "Is this the Mariazell Basilica?" I asked.

"Oh my, no darling. It's the Schönbrunn Palace." Zelda whispered, "Isn't it magical, Miss Jade Fair? Close your eyes, darling. Let your many hopes and dreams surround you."

Her voice seemed to command me to follow her instructions. Not in a demanding way, but in a way that I wanted to please her. I closed my eyes as if my eyelids were no longer in my control.

"Can you see yourself there?" Zelda whispered.

I nodded. I needed an escape from mourning Sully's passing, even a temporary one, so I pictured myself standing in front of the palace.

"Envision it. Envision it Miss Jade Fair. Envision yourself standing right in front of that magnificent palace. Take in the splendor of it all." Zelda's whispered words became faint as if traveling away from me.

I felt a rush of warm air followed by a frigid blast. I assumed someone must have opened the shop's door, but I was unwilling or maybe unable to open my eyes to see who had entered. Following Zelda's melodious voice, I continued to wish I was in Vienna in front of that magnificent palace.

My right eye fluttered. And then the fluttering of my right eye transformed to outright twitching followed by my left eye imitating my right. My shallow breathing felt as if something had sucked most of the oxygen out of my lungs. My heart pounded so vigorously I thought I might have been having a heart attack. As internally freaked out as I was by this rush of uncontrollable eye movements and heart pounding, my body remained as motionless as the statue in Spring Creek's town gardens.

The eye twitching ended as rapidly as it had begun, and everything became still with deafening silence. Then, something soft, cold, and wet caressed my cheeks while soft murmurings of distant conversations descended into the silence.

I allowed my right eye to peek open ever so slightly. I was clearly not in Spring Creek anymore.

****

Vienna, Austria 1917

A tall slender man towered over a petite girl with long flowing brown waves caressing her cheeks. Even with a heavy wool-like overcoat, I could tell he had broad shoulders and a slim build. Snow gently descended around them, turning the girl's violet cap almost completely white. The rim of the man's homburg looked as if someone had sprinkled an entire bag of flour onto it.

He stooped down nearer to her height. They both gazed up at the huge palace. "This is the Schönbrunn Palace, Lilloise," he spoke in a soft tone as gentle as the snow falling around them.

I could no longer hear Zelda's voice, but only the conversation of the man and girl.

"Look at its magnificence." He pointed toward the palace with an outstretched arm.

"There are so many windows, Papa," Lilloise spoke with delight in her voice. "How many, Papa?" A muffled sound came from her mittened hands clapping. She turned toward him and hugged her Papa around his neck.

I would have loved to have had Sully in my life when I was young like this little Lilloise. But I'd been robbed of making such lovely memories.

I marveled at the palace with its white façade which I guessed was granite. The little girl was correct, there were numerous windows. Too many to count. I turned to see several figures in the middle of a silent fountain. They were frozen just like the ice surrounding them. Neptune appeared to be one of the sculptures standing high above the rest. I shivered.

I suddenly remembered that none of it was real. *This is getting creepy.* It was as if I were there. I did not like the feeling of not being in control. *Was Zelda manipulating my mind?* My heart's pounding echoed in my ears while it felt as if my heart were about to leap out of my chest. Her apparent mind game elevated to frightening.

"Zelda," I shrieked.

They turned toward me and stared. Lilloise pointed her mittened hand toward me.

They'd heard me.

I opened my eyes and Zelda had the snow globe in her hands. I was back in the Weary Traveler's Antique Treasures, frightened and confused.

Chapter Two

Spring Creek 2011

"You're quivering my dear." Zelda placed the globe back in the empty spot among its many neighbors. "Come sit here." She placed her hand on my elbow and guided me toward a nearby settee.

Still confused by what had happened, I stuttered, "I, I, I, need to get to work." I resisted her offer to sit because I had an immediate urge to run. I had never felt both giddy and frightened simultaneously. That mixture unnerved me.

"Oh, my darling. Are you frightened by thunderstorms?"

My eyes widened as my look said, 'Are you kidding me? It's not the storm frightening me. You've just messed with my brain!' I inched toward the door.

"I wish you would stay until you've stopped shaking." Zelda followed closely. "I can make you a cup of my blended chamomile tea. It's very soothing."

"No. I really do need to get to work." I didn't quite know what had happened, but I needed to escape before a full-scale anxiety attack surfaced. *Besides, I'd never trust this woman's tea concoction.*

"The storm has slowed to just a drizzle, but you'll still need an umbrella to stay dry." Zelda handed me an umbrella with whimsical cats donning straw hats covering the entire purple fabric. "No hurry getting it back to me. We have many others."

I thanked her, grabbed the feline-covered umbrella, and dashed out the door. The bell above the entrance rang violently. It warned, "Hurry. Get out while you can!"

Maybe no one will notice since I'm only twenty minutes late. I inhaled the rain-filtered air, grabbed the door handle just below the golden letters on the door of Gladman, Avery, & Burke, Attorneys at Law, and prepared to face the consequences of a morning spun out of my control.

The first person I ran into was a co-worker, Carl. "You look awful, Jade!" She studied my face. "Are you feeling all right?"

Carl had joined our office about six months ago. When Carl was sixteen and applying for a driver's license, she had presented her birth certificate for proof of age. That was when she realized the hospital had left off the "y" in her name, Carly. For sixteen years she went by Carly. She could have had it legally changed to what her parents had chosen, but quirky Carly decided it would be cool to use the misspelled name. She reveled in the fact that her name surprised people. A tall curvy twenty-two-year-old young lady with a mane of silky jet-black hair sporting a swath of cobalt blue occupying the bottom third. She presented herself as outgoing and always in search of the next party.

We'd had an instant connection because of our joint misery of working at the law firm. However, that was the only thing we had in common. She was about eight years younger and a frequent visitor to Embersville, two towns over. Every Monday she would recount her "fantastic" weekend, which included Embersville's best bars and live music. Not really my thing – loved the music, hated crowded bars.

"Winnie!" Carl placed her body directly in front of me, so that I could not advance. "Winnie! Come take a look at Jade. She looks awful. No, it's worse than awful. She looks absolutely dreadful!" Carl crossed her arms ninja style revealing a small dove tattoo with the word *Lovely* in small script letters just below the bird.

"I'll be okay. Just give me a minute." I swiped at the perspiration above my lip.

"It'll take more than a minute. Your blouse is untucked, you're shivering, and you are sweating profusely. You are not your usual put-together self."

Of course, I looked disheveled. I'd endured the stress of Sully's memorial, was zombie- walking on a few hours of sleep, and some red-headed wacky lady terrified me with some mind game or maybe some newfangled sorcery or some such nonsense.

"You need to go home, girly." Winnie stopped abruptly when she neared me and then backed up two steps. "You're sweating and shaking. You might be downright contagious!"

Winnie's our work mom. Free with advice, sometimes solicited and most times not. But always the peacemaker. She had covered for my lateness more times than she should have.

"I'll be fine. I'll go to the ladies' room and pull myself together." I forced a smile to convince her and myself.

"It does not look like you'll be able to—" and with air quotes, she added, "—pull yourself together." Winnie shook her head. "You're definitely coming down with something."

I knew I wasn't 'coming down with something' but I also knew I wasn't in the head space to make it through the day.

"Mr. Avery's not in yet. Had a meeting at the main office in Embersville." Winnie backed up a few more steps. "I'll tell him you were sick and needed to go home."

I scanned the room for Jessica, the person who could not wait to tell on co-workers for the tiniest infraction. Every office has one.

"You're in luck." Winnie winked. "Avery took her with him. Mr. Burke and Mr. Gladman are also offsite."

Unintentionally, my sigh of relief sounded more like a groan, remnants of a past run-in with Jessica.

Winnie raised an eyebrow and shooed me with her hands. "Now get going before we all catch whatever this here thing is you have."

"You look awful!" Carl repeated. "Shit! You look worse than awful! Never seen put-together Jade looking like this." Carl waved her arms up and down the outline of my figure.

"Okay, Carl. Don't make her feel worse than she already is." Winnie cautioned.

I did not feel awful. I did not even feel sick, just a little shaken. I was, however, still trying to wrap my head around what had happened at Zelda's antique shop. I had been so dazed and upset after the incident; I had hurried out of there before I could process anything because my concern pivoted to fear of getting fired. And to make matters worse, I left my coffee at Zelda's store.

Because of their appalled looks and their alarming vocalizations, I realized I must not have disguised my distress very well. So, I took Winnie's advice and headed for home. But before I left, I stopped by my cubicle and grabbed the spare jacket hanging from my chair even though the rain seemed to have stopped.

On my hasty trip toward home, I crossed over to the other side of the street and looked straight ahead when passing by Zelda's shop. I did not want to chance running into her and potentially risking a repeat encounter.

I was just one block from my apartment when the sky released yet another downpour. A steadfast rule of mine was that I never ran in the rain. Because if I slipped and fell, I would not only be wet, but I would also be wet and injured.

Soaked from head to toe, including my favorite yellow leather slip-ons, I climbed the stairs of the old Victorian converted into three separate apartments. Mine sat at the very top. I liked to think of it as a penthouse, when in reality it was an attic space renovated into an efficiency apartment.

Don't know why people refer to them as efficient. Mine was so small, I had no room to organize anything. However, I tried to think of it as cozy and snug. Those two euphemisms helped me to accept my plight—a thirty-year-old, in a small town, so small it was hard to take a breath, living in a twenty-five by twenty-foot box with an uncomfortable pull-out couch for a bed that must have been previously used as a torture implement to get information from innocent victims.

After I peeled off one sleeve of my rain-soaked jacket, it was apparent that not only my shoes, but also my new silk blouse had turned out to be collateral damage. To make the day worse, I realized I still had the hat-wearing feline umbrella clutched tightly in my other hand.

"What a loser." It had never occurred to me to open it during the last downpour. My words reverberated around the tiny room. "Mom was right when she'd said I'd never amount to much." I threw down the umbrella, wrestled off the remaining sleeve of my jacket, and collapsed onto a stool in my kitchenette.

The raindrops blended with my expensive hair gel which I had applied that morning onto my spiraling dark brown curls. The droplets mixture traveled down my forehead and into my eyes and then merged with overflowing tears. They formed a waterfall which streamed from my chin. Instead of focusing on the hair product stinging my eyes, I lamented on the money wasted on product being washed away.

I swiped the wet away from my chin and mumbled to the empty room, "Can my life be any more pathetic?"

I shuffled to the bathroom, shed my drenched clothes, and reached for my robe. My chilled skin welcomed the fluffy dry terry cloth fabric, the only good thing so far that day. Wrapped around me, my pink robe felt like a warm hug.

On a sticky note, clinging to the mirror, I had placed a reminder that read, *Let go of the past. It serves no purpose.* I recited the affirmation every morning and each evening, repeated the words, "It serves no purpose. It serves no purpose. It serves no purpose."

Those were Sully's words. It had amazed me that he hadn't felt any hatred toward my mother for keeping me a secret from him. He had said that he was blessed that he had gotten to meet me and had the opportunity as well to get to know me. I, on the other hand, struggled to forgive her.

I reread the words and repeated them aloud, but the reflection in the mirror above the bathroom sink stared back at me.

She said, "If you look up pathetic in the dictionary, you will find a picture of Jade Fair." As much as I tried to overcome my self-doubt, I feared that the woman in the mirror spoke the truth.

Coffee was my downfall in the morning, but tea was my evening comfort. Although it was technically still morning, I needed a cup of cozy comfort. I plodded in my matching pink terry slippers to my tiny kitchenette, made a cup of my favorite hot drink, Tea Forte's Breakfast Blend. It was more expensive than my budget allowed, so I only used it on occasions when there was something to celebrate or when I needed extra relaxation. Otherwise, I used a tea bag from the box of one-hundred count generic blend from Greene's Market.

The events of that day definitely called for the more expensive blend. After brewing a perfect cup, I slumped into my well-worn but still comfy recliner I had inherited from the previous tenant.

I reviewed the weird events from the morning. "If I can't sort out what had happened at the antique store, I'll have to resign myself to the fact that I've lost my mind and will need extensive therapy … which I cannot afford." I spoke as if someone was listening, cared about my troubles, and would offer meaningful solutions.

My first reaction to the occurrence in Zelda's store had been that she had messed with my brain. However, after giving it some thought, I questioned if it had really happened. Then I flipped to thinking that something certainly had happened. And once again questioned that maybe I was being a bit too dramatic. Or had I experienced some sort of unexplainable episode?

Confusion swarmed in my brain like a bunch of bees at a picnic. The many chaotic thoughts took up all available space, and I could not produce a logical conclusion. Unless I'd had a major breakdown, I was certain a time portal was ridiculously impossible. If it was some sort of episode, I couldn't quite put a name to it, so I grabbed a notepad and listed all reasonable options.

> I had temporarily passed out and it had been a
> dream.
> I had suffered from narcolepsy, momentarily fell
> asleep, and had dreamt the whole thing.
> It had been just a very vivid daydream.
> Someone had spiked my coffee with a
> hallucinogenic drug.
> Zelda had hypnotized me.

The last one on the list was most likely a possibility, but also the scariest. Or, and it was a very big or, it really had happened. I had traveled, though briefly, to another place and possibly another time. Although the scene with the man and girl

26

was serene and calming, it was still frightening to not be in control. Ultimately, the list generated more questions than answers.

The only thing I knew for sure was that I really needed Sully. I had no one to confide in. I hadn't spoken to my mother or stepfather in years, my half-brother, Will and I had a very strained relationship, and close friendships were nonexistent. Since Sully's death, I had been treading water barely holding my head above the waves, but after the unexplainable events of that morning, the waves were winning.

Will had once asked why I was so bitter. He had also added his unsolicited opinion that self-doubt was not a good look on me. I never answered him because I thought it was obvious. Mom had always treated him like he could do no wrong because he excelled in school and my stepdad, his biological dad, and Will had so much in common because they both were consumed with sports.

I shook my head in an attempt to shake Will's past words from echoing in my brain because I did not want to admit that his words might possibly be true. I closed my eyes attempting to escape the craziness of my morning, but images of the man and girl appeared as vibrant as if I was there again. *Think of something positive. Think of something positive. Think of something positive.*

Slowly my pursed lips transformed into a smile. Even though Mondays were not my volunteer time at the animal shelter, I would go anyway. The dogs always welcomed me with kisses and incessant tail wags. Especially the tiny brown scrawny one they had named The Beast because he had growled at everyone who had tried to approach him. They had almost put him down because of his temperament, but he had responded to my voice and had allowed me to approach him. He had eventually taken a treat from my hand and had even permitted me to pet him. Once he had trusted me, he slowly trusted the other workers. I would have liked to have adopted him, but my landlord did not permit pets of any kind.

Thinking of The Beast persuaded the muscle tension to leave my neck and shoulders and subside from the rest of my body. Relaxation and one more sip of tea enabled me to temporarily drift far away from my negative thoughts and worries.

Chapter Three

Spring Creek 2011

Awakened from a sound sleep to rhythmic tapping, I scanned the room attempting to make sense of where I was. Then I heard my name faintly called. "Jade. Jade. It's me."

More tapping and the muffled voice became slightly louder and clearer. "Jade. Jade. It's Winnie."

"Winnie? What are you doing here?" I scrambled from the recliner. "Wait a second. I'll let you in."

"No. No girly. I don't want to catch whatever you have."

That's when everything from that morning came flooding back—the storm, Zelda's probable mind game, worried co-workers.

Before I opened the door, I straightened the stack of books on my coffee table, shoved a pile of papers under the couch, and moved the breakfast dishes from the counter to the sink. I tightened my robe and unlocked the door. Winnie backed up when I opened it.

"I brought you soup. Chicken noodle from The Little Red Barn diner. It's in that bag, right there on the landing next to your door."

"Thanks. But actually, I don't have anything you can catch. I think I might have had a panic attack. Come on in."

Winnie hesitated and then came a little closer probably to inspect me and make sure. "You still look frightful."

I was sure frizz had dominated my hair from sleeping on it when wet. Knowing my mane could not be easily tamed, I grabbed a scarf from the coat hook and quickly wrapped it around my head. I opened the door wider and invited her in with a sweep of my arm. Still hesitant, she only took two steps into my apartment.

"Seriously. You can't catch anything from me. Have a seat. I'll make us some tea."

"Do you have any beer? It was a long day at the firm."

I realized I'd slept the entire day away, and Winnie must have been on her way home from work instead of what I had originally thought of as her lunch break.

"Avery and Jessica returned to the office with some crazy ideas they'd like to implement." Winnie took the bottle of beer from me and waved away the glass. "I'm certain he took her to the meeting at the firm's main office because as you know, she will do anything to gain favor which includes agreeing with everything he says and does."

I nodded.

"And it's gone to her head." Winnie took a swig of beer. "You know I'm always in favor of a peaceful work environment, but I'll put her in her place. I'm not afraid of her antics."

Thoughts of Jessica gaining more power caused a shudder to run from one shoulder to the other. Just when I thought my day couldn't get any worse, it did. I passed unhappy and soared straight to desperate – desperate to find a new job preferably away from Spring Creek. My mind wandered to thoughts of winning the lottery, buying a reliable car, and driving out of town to anywhere, anywhere except Pittsburgh's Shadyside.

"Jade, are you sure you're all right?"

"Yes. Sorry. Just caught up in my thoughts."

Winnie wrinkled her nose, squinted one eye, and tilted her head. "Did something happen to cause you to have a panic attack?"

I smiled to try to convince her and me that I was okay. I changed the subject, "I didn't know you knew where I lived."

"Carl told me. She said she'd only been here once, so she wasn't exactly sure but surprisingly gave me fairly accurate directions." Winnie looked around. "Well, this is quite cozy. Plenty of room for one person."

I forced a smile. Like she wasn't saying out loud everything I already knew. Cozy was a synonym for small and cheap. And 'plenty of room for one person.' was the same as saying all alone with nobody who cared.

"Do you have any family around that maybe could look in on you?"

"Not really," I shrugged. "No worries, Winnie. I'll be fine. I had a nice long nap and now I have this wonderful smelling soup."

I realized I had been working with Winnie for almost three years and she knew very little about me and vice versa. Up until that point, we'd never been to each other's homes or done anything together outside of work. Most times, we didn't even have lunch together. Several times she had invited me to events outside of work, but I usually invented excuses for why I couldn't attend or join in. I liked my privacy and despised when people judged me especially by circumstances out of my control. But sometimes, I wished I had not made so many excuses.

Sully had been the only reason I had moved to Spring Creek, and in addition to being my father, he was the only friend I needed and trusted. Since he had been gone, grief had converted loving memories into painful ones, and I was still hesitant to let myself be vulnerable again.

"Jade! Are you caught up in your thoughts again?" Winnie stared at me with genuine concern emblazoned across her face. "You look like you are a million miles away."

"Actually, only two," I sighed remembering how close I had once lived to him. Whenever possible, I avoided going anywhere near where he used to live, where we had made so many perfect memories in such a short amount of time.

Winnie looked confused. "I understand if it's too personal, but do you want to talk about what caused a panic attack?" Winnie persisted.

I desperately wanted to confide in what I believed triggered it but knew I could never share what had happened in the antique store. That would have been too embarrassing admitting that I had allowed someone control of my mind or whatever that had been.

Winnie was the type of mom I had always dreamed of having. I desperately wanted to trust someone, which I had not done since Sully. So, I gave her a little snippet of recent events, careful to leave out that morning's incident.

"I'm sure you already know I'm not happy at the law firm. Jessica has it in for me and has welcomed Mr. Avery into her fold. In addition to that, the work is less than fulfilling."

Winnie nodded. "I think Carl feels the same. That's why I always try to be a buffer for you girls."

When I was a young girl, I would lie in bed at night pretending I had a mother who would stick up for me and be proud of me. I'd imagined her as a good listener and funny, too. If my younger self's imagination had come to life, my imaginary mother would be a lot like Winnie.

"I'm sorry I've never thanked you because I really do appreciate that." I sucked in air deep into my lungs to summon even a small bit of courage and to stop my hands from shaking. "My father passed away a few months back and yesterday was his memorial service."

Winnie left her beer on the counter and walked to me. "I'm so sorry, dear." She patted my hands. "I wish I'd have known. I would have been there for you. I'm sure Carl would have, too."

As difficult as it was to open up to her, I felt a sense of relief. I'd had several conversations with Sully concerning my lack of close friendships. Even though he had understood why I mistrusted people, he had still encouraged me saying, "I won't be around forever." At the time, I had not realized how soon his words would come true.

"Surely that was the cause of your panic attack this morning. Grief can trigger a multitude of issues."

She had no idea what the combination of grief combined with a wacky red head could do to a person's psyche.

"I don't mean to pry, but don't you have anyone who could look in on you?"

I shook my head.

"Write this down." She motioned writing with an invisible pen using her palm as the paper."

I searched through a drawer in my kitchenette for a pad of paper and a pen and then wrote as she dictated her cell phone number, her landline phone number, and her husband's cell number. Winnie was definitely thorough.

"Do not hesitate to call or text any one of those numbers." She pointed her finger at me. She probably guessed that I might be unwilling to do so.

"I'll see you at work tomorrow." She paused. "I am concerned about the upcoming weekend, though. Jim and I are going to the cabin and cell service is pretty sketchy. I'll make sure you get Carl's cell number, too. Just in case you need someone when I'm not available."

"I'm sure it was a single event." I said aloud as I tried to convince her and hopefully convince myself. "Thank you again for the soup and also for your concern."

Winnie gave me a quick shoulder squeeze. I guessed I had convinced her that it definitely was a panic attack and that I was not contagious.

"I'll see you tomorrow." I returned her squeeze with an attempt at a hug. "And I promise I'll call if I need to." At that moment, I realized that I had taken the first step toward establishing a friendship. I smiled knowing I would have made Sully happy.

Chapter Four

Spring Creek 2011

For once, old Ronnie Dante's forecast was spot on. He predicted a "gorgeous day." It was a sunny sea-blue sky kind of day. Even better, it was Saturday. Two days devoid of sitting in a stuffy office with Mr. Avery's accusatory glances, and Jessica's spite-filled stares.

Determined to get better at healthy choices, I had decided that it was a great day to burn some extra calories and take a walk to the park. Zelda's umbrella sat perched in the corner near my apartment door. I reluctantly tucked it under my arm. "I guess I should get this back to her," I mumbled on my way out. Her store was only a few blocks from the park. *Maybe she'll be off at another auction, and I'll be able to just hang it on the doorknob.*

I finally concluded that the incident at Zelda's was a weird anomaly and that I had probably allowed my imagination to distort reality way out of proportion. I was determined to cleanse my thoughts of what had happened at the antique store and never speak of it to anyone. Although, I couldn't seem to completely eradicate little Lilloise and her soft-spoken papa from occasionally sneaking

36

into my thoughts. I imagined different scenarios contemplating their lives in Austria. I would be mortified if anyone knew I felt a kindred connection to two non-existent people.

Umbrella and self-assurance in hand, I walked down Main Street and hummed a made-up tune, an extreme contrast to my previous visit. Time, a little distance, and self-reflection guided my out-of-control imagination into the proper perspective. As I got closer to the store, I decided just to be safe, I would not linger. I'd just return the umbrella, thank her, and be on my way. I especially would not let her hypnotize me again.

Standing in front of her door, a bit of nervousness crept into my thoughts. Hoping to calm my last-minute apprehension, I inhaled all available air my lungs could possibly hold, and slowly turned the knob. Warily, I stepped inside. The bell above the door announced my arrival, and to my surprise it sounded not as ominous as it had the day before. It practically chimed, "Welcome." *See Jade! You were definitely letting your imagination run wild.*

Zelda was behind the counter, cell phone peeking out from her wild red spikey hair. I placed the umbrella onto the counter, mouthed thank you, quickly turned, and headed toward the door. As soon as I reached the door, I let out my breath I hadn't realized I had been holding.

Hand on the doorknob, I was two steps away from the sidewalk to freedom when my ears betrayed me. "Jade! Jade Fair!"

My head drooped. I could not be rude, so I turned to face her. Zelda scurried toward me. "Oh, darling. It's so nice to see you."

"Zelda. Hi. I didn't want to disturb you while you were on the phone. Just wanted to return your umbrella. Thanks so much." The words spilled out in one short breath. I turned again to leave, but Zelda caught my elbow.

"I must show you something," she said in a child-like voice as if excited for her first pony ride.

My heart sank. I was going to have to be firm and escape as quickly as possible. "I really can't stay." I mustered a strong voice.

She persisted, "I want to show you a few more of the snow globes I've unpacked since your last visit here."

She left me standing there just inches from the door. The knots returned to my stomach, my breath tightened in my throat, and a sharp lump formed.

Zelda returned as quickly as she had left. She carried an ornately decorated globe smaller than any of the others. "This one is my new favorite. It's from Paris!"

I was drawn to the beautiful carvings around the base and the gold leafing which highlighted the etchings. The snow formed around the base of the miniature Louvre as if it had been built on a frothy cloud. The globe must have been purchased years ago as the Pei glass pyramid was not present in the courtyard.

A trip to Paris was something I'd always imagined I'd do one day. I romanticized it in my daydreams. I'd even purchased an English-to-French dictionary and addressed my apartment each time I left or came home. To my couch, chair, and tiny apartment I would say, "*au revoir canape, au revoir chaise, au revoir petit appartement.*" And when I returned, "*bonjour canape, bonjour chaise, bonjour petit appartement.*"

Zelda grasped my hands and placed the globe firmly in my grip, jolting me from my thoughts. "Isn't it beautiful!" She rocked my hands and the snow globe gently back and forth. "Wouldn't you love to travel to Paris, Jade Fair? It would be divine, fascinating, enchanting. Yes, enchanting to travel there, wouldn't it? Wouldn't it, Jade Fair? Think of it darling. Travel to Paris—a most romantic city." She continued to move the globe seemingly glued in my grip while my feet remained frozen in place. The imitation snow fell gently around the former palace and mesmerized my thoughts. It seemed so real.

No, no, no. She's doing it again and I'm unable to resist.

****

Paris, France 1927
In front of the Louvre Museum

"*Merci. Merci. Merci*. Thank you, Marguerite. This has been the best birthday ever!"

"Lilloise, you only turn sixteen once, so I wanted to ensure it would be memorable." Marguerite placed into Lilloise's hands a snow globe with ornate carvings around the base etched in gold. "This is so you will always remember me and our special time together here in Paris."

Could this be little Lilloise? The same girl I saw in front of the Schönbrunn Palace? She's taller and nearly a young woman.

"I could never forget you." A tear slid down Lilloise's cheek.

"Why the tears? This is your special day. No sad thoughts." Marguerite wiped the tear from Lilloise's face and replaced it with a gentle kiss.

"I can't believe we're leaving for the States in two days. I may never see you again." Lilloise reached for Marguerite's hand.

"*Non! Belle amie*." Marguerite held Lilloise's face in her hands. "We will write to each other every day, my beautiful friend."

"You will always have a piece of my heart." Lilloise touched her forehead and nose to Marguerite's.

"This is not goodbye." Marguerite curled Lilloise's hair around her finger. "*Nous nous reverrons*—We will meet again."

Lilloise whispered. "*Je t'aime.*"

"*Je t'aime aussi.*" Marguerite replied and then whispered, "I love you, too."

A harsh male voice startled me. "Lilloise! Time to go. Say your goodbyes, quickly." I recognized the man. I was certain it was Lilloise's papa. Still tall and slim, but he had aged several years. His tone was curt and brusque, quite the contrast from the soft-spoken man I'd remembered from my previously envisioned journey to Austria.

Marguerite stole a final hug and whispered, "*Au revoir pour l'instant.*"

"For now," replied Lilloise. She clutched the snow globe to her heart. I recognized it as the same one Zelda had just placed into my hands.

Lilloise winced as Papa grabbed her arm and escorted her away from the embrace she'd shared with Marguerite. Standing alone staring after them, Marguerite was now the one wiping tears from her own face.

Compassion swelled in my soul as I remembered my own heart-wrenching experience of having to say goodbye to a dear friend. "I'm sorry," I whispered.

Marguerite spun toward me. Her tear-filled eyes met mine. I said aloud, "I'm so sorry."

"Why are you sorry, dear?" It was Zelda. She was holding the globe.

I shook my head and bolted for the door.

Chapter Five

Spring Creek 2011

"How was your weekend, Jade?" Winnie looked up from her computer. "And how are you feeling?"

"I'm feeling much better. And my weekend, it was…" I paused to come up with an appropriate description, "interesting."

"Interesting! Hmm." Winnie winked.

"I'm sure your imagination is much more exciting than my weekend actually was." I tossed my jacket over her head.

"Air conditioning is brutal today. They've obviously forgotten to turn it to off. You'll need this." Winnie handed my jacket back to me.

Before she had the chance to ask me to elaborate on my interesting weekend and to avoid sharing, I asked her, "How was your weekend at camp with Jim?"

"Well, it's camp. I wish I could relax like Jim does the minute we step onto the cabin's front porch." She shrugged. "But there's still cooking, cleaning, and any necessary repairs to do there. Jim is in his element in nature, so he doesn't seem to mind any of the chores. And I always think of the millions of things waiting for me at home."

"I see your point." I paused to think of another way to steer the conversation away from me, but I'd hesitated too long.

"Care to share details of your interesting weekend?" Winnie's expression bordered on devious.

"No. But thank you for asking." I grimaced while I reminded myself of the events of Saturday. When it happened once, I'd dismissed it, as maybe I was mistaken. But when it had occurred the second time, it went way past 'maybe I was mistaken' and traveled like a bullet train straight to 'it undeniably occurred.'

"You are one mysterious person." Winnie nodded as if agreeing with herself.

Carl twirled past us. "Let your imagination go wild on my weekend," she shrieked.

"Another one of those, heh, Carl?" Winnie shook her head, disappointment oozing from each word.

"Oh, Winnie," Carl gave her a hug. "You were young once. Weren't you?" Sarcasm hung onto each word. "Although it's hard for me to picture it," Carl chided.

"I wish you could see into the future and know the effects of your choices." Winnie tapped at her keyboard. "Right, Jade?"

I thought about Winnie's words "effects of your choices." Most times in my life things had happened that were not my choices—rather they were events out of my control. I did not choose to have a mother who had kept my biological father from me. I did not choose for him to have died so soon after I had met him. I did not choose to have had relationships end in disasters and friends who had disappeared completely from my life.

"Right, Jade?" Winnie stopped typing and looked up at me.

"I'm not picking sides." I was the most unqualified person to give advice on life choices.

"What's a twenty-two-year-old woman to do for fun in this little rinky-dink town?" Carl pointed first at me and then at Winnie. "Well, you tell me what I should do for fun."

"I'll tell you what, Miss Carly Mae Hutchinson." Winnie grabbed Carl's finger. "Jim is going out of town this weekend for a reunion with his old Army buddies."

Carl backed away and folded her arms as if waiting for a prison sentence.

"Hear me out." Winnie placed her hands on her hips. "I haven't shared my idea yet."

Carl tapped her foot, arms still folded seeming to prejudge the fifty-eight-year-old woman's impending suggestion. "I'm listening."

"If Jade will join us, we'll have an old-fashioned sleepover." Winnie's smile spread across her face.

I remembered once overhearing the popular girls in my sixth-grade class talking about a sleepover one of them was having. I had so desperately longed to be a part of that group. I never was.

Then toward the end of the school year, a new girl joined our class. Her name was Tiffany. We became best of friends. We were inseparable doing everything together. We had several sleepovers where we'd talk late into the night. We knew all the words to Whitney Houston's, *I'm Every Woman* and had sung into hairbrushes, pretending they were microphones. Tiffany's mom would call upstairs to tell us to go to sleep. We giggled and then had silently mouth the words to the song.

Sometimes, even after spending an entire day together, we would then go to our respective homes and call each other on our home phones talking for another hour. The next school year in seventh grade, we had advanced to a new school building and fortunately had the same schedule. I had been relieved to have a friend in each class and a lunch buddy.

Then it happened. Near the end of the school year, she told me that she and her family were moving to Texas because of her father's job. The day she moved was the worst. I had lost my best friend, my confidant, and the person I had regarded as the sister I'd always wanted.

Since we did not have cell phones back then, every phone call required a very expensive long-distance fee. We had attempted to keep in touch by writing letters, but eventually that had faded.

"Jade, Jade, what do you say? Are you in?" Winnie looked from me to Carl. "Are you both in?"

"Aren't we a little old for sleepovers?" Carl did not seem convinced.

"I have a well-stocked fridge and bar." Winnie sang the word bar.

"Now you're talking." Carl clapped. "The Embersville bars can get along without me for one weekend. I'm in!"

With raised eyebrows, Winnie looked at me. "What about you, Jade?"

Sully's words of concern about me not having any close friends echoed in my head. I whispered, "I'm in too." Maybe it was him nudging me to take a tiny step toward connecting with these two ladies and becoming more than just co-workers.

The rest of the week was rather uneventful. We decided to have our sleepover on Saturday since we had all agreed that by Friday, we were usually exhausted.

Getting ready for the get-together brought back happy memories of time spent with Tiffany. I hoped there might be a chance I possibly could forge the same type of friendship with Carl and Winnie. Even though I was hesitant to transition from work colleagues to friends, I could feel Sully's encouragement. The thought of him by my side eased the constant fear that they might not accept me if they knew the whole truth about me. So, I shoved my fears aside and decided I'd share only if necessary.

Since I usually slept in sweats and t-shirts, I drove to Embersville Saturday morning to The Emporium Department

Store to purchase a cute pink pajama set and new pink fluffy slippers to match my robe. I also stopped by Greene's Market to pick up a few indulgent snacks. Then I purchased two bottles of wine and a six-pack of beer since that was Winnie's preferred drink. I knew a little about Winnie since she had shared snippets of her life during work breaks, but I knew practically nothing about Carl other than her escapades in Embersville. I hoped she liked beer or wine.

I arrived at Winnie's address a little after seven o'clock, the time we had agreed upon. Perched on the front porch steps was Carl, her sleeping bag, and an overstuffed backpack.

"Why are you out here?" I asked. "Where's Winnie?"

"I have no idea. I've knocked several times with no answer." Carl stood to face me. "I texted her and even called her cell number several times, but she did not reply or answer."

I pulled out my cellphone to check the time. "I'm a little worried. This is so unlike reliable Winnie."

"I'm hoping she made a quick trip to the grocery store and got hung up in traffic."

"Ha-ha. Traffic in Spring Creek." I shook my head. "Not likely."

"You're right. Have a seat while we wait for her." Carl slid her gear over to make room for me.

"Let's sit up there." I pointed to the two rocking chairs on the porch. "It'll be more comfortable than those stairs."

I set my bags on a wicker table and slid onto a rocker. Carl joined me. "Whatcha got in that big bag?"

"Beer, wine, and some snacks."

"You came prepared." She pointed to her backpack. "I only brought some snacks."

While waiting for Winnie, we discussed the possibility of Mr. Avery's proposed changes coming to fruition. But that conversation immediately dragged down our moods. So, we shifted the chat to something more lighthearted and pleasant. Carl shared about a country band she'd been following who sometimes played at one of the bars in Embersville. I told her about the novel I had been reading and TV programs I was addicted to, nothing too personal. After about a half an hour, Winnie finally pulled up in her Jeep.

"Winnie! Where have you been?" Carl jumped up, ran down the steps, and met her on the sidewalk.

Winnie burst into tears. My foundation was rocked by the sight of Winnie, the strongest person I knew, displaying such raw emotion. I blinked away the tears that had formed in my eyes, a reaction to seeing her so emotional. Then I scurried down the steps and put my arms around her. She sobbed into my shoulder. Carl took her hand, and we led her to the porch. Winnie shook so badly she could not unlock the front door. Carl got the door open, and the three of us entered and sat on the couch with Winnie between us.

When she was calm enough to talk, she said, "It's Jim." She caught her breath. "He's had a stroke." Winnie wrung her hands as if she were applying hand cream.

"I'm so sorry." I put my arm around her. Images of Sully after his stroke caused tears to again well up in my eyes. This time, I could not blink them away.

On her other side, Carl echoed, "So sorry." And then asked, "What can we do for you?"

"I'm just here to grab a few things. I'm going to spend the night at the hospital." Winnie shook her head. "He's my everything, my rock. It's unbearable seeing him so helpless."

Visions of my dad in the hospital bed, tubes, strange beeps, and the awful smell of death streamed back into my thoughts. I shuddered. "Don't think like that, Winnie. We're here for you. Call or text me anytime."

After Winnie had gathered a few things, we walked her to her car, gave her hugs, and watched her drive off.

"It's unsettling seeing her like that." Carl sighed. "She's always the strong one."

"I could use a drink." I pointed to my bags still on the porch. "Care to join me for a beer or perhaps wine?"

"I'm a whiskey girl. Let's go to my place." Carl pointed down the street. "It's not too far from here."

"I'll follow you."

On the short drive, I could not shake the image of even-keeled Winnie trembling and sobbing. It was unsettling, and I could not blink it away. I ached for her and worse yet seeing her like that brought back the broken heartedness I had felt when I lost Sully. It felt as real as if it had just happened. When Winnie spoke the word 'stroke' it grabbed me as if I had unexpectedly driven off a cliff that I had not noticed in front of me. Without warning, I crashed. And my heart, which had been trying to heal, received another sizeable tear.

We arrived at Carl's, and I told myself to shake it off. This wasn't about me. This was two coworkers getting together to hopefully figure out how we could be of help to Winnie.

Chapter Six

Spring Creek 2011

Carl's place was not what I had expected. It was a huge Victorian. Even in the late evening dusk I could see that it was well maintained, no faded and peeling paint like the one I inhabited. I assumed it was converted, and she had one of the levels like mine. We entered through the beveled glass front door. Carl kicked off her boots and said, "Welcome to my humble abode."

"So, you have the whole first floor?" I did not try to hide the jealousy in my tone.

"No," Carl chuckled. "I have the whole house, all three floors." She threw her hands above her head.

Shock spread from my chin to my forehead which wrinkled into my hairline.

"It's only temporary." Carl sighed. "Michael, my wealthy ex-boyfriend, had paid the entire year's rent. It's a long story."

"We've got all evening, and I'm all ears." I was grateful that if she took up the entire evening telling her tale of woe, then the pressure would be off me to share.

My head swiveled as if I was watching a tennis match. I could not take my eyes off the beautiful, raised-panel wainscoting adorning the walls, the lofty ceilings, and ornate marble inlaid floors. And we were only in the entrance.

"Well let's get those drinks first, and then we can chat." She led me down a long cherry wood-paneled hall with stained glass sconces lighting the way.

I followed her into an enormous kitchen. It had original-looking slate floors, and massive built-in beveled glass cabinets. I estimated the walls scaled at least fourteen feet reaching up to an intricate tin ceiling. The countertops were solid white marble with subtle grey veining. Her kitchen was larger than my entire apartment.

"Wine, beer, whiskey, or…" Carl shimmied as she sang the last word, "tequila?" She placed two glasses on an immense antique table taking up residence in the center of the kitchen.

"I'll have Cabernet." I pulled the bottle from my bag.

"Huh. I pegged you for a Chardonnay girl." Carl replaced one of the glasses with a flowery-etched goblet and uncorked the wine bottle.

"Actually, I'm more of a tea drinker." I shrugged. "But I need a drink. Seeing Winnie like that really shook me. Besides, I didn't want you to have to drink alone."

"I appreciate that. But I'm used to drinking alone. Doesn't really bother me much."

53

There was sadness in Carl's voice that failed to match her flippant words. She filled my wine goblet; an amount I was sure I would not be able to finish without my head spinning. For herself, and without measuring, she poured from a bottle of Tullamore Dew Irish whiskey, added some cranberry juice, squeezed half a lime, and then to that she added a few other ingredients which I was not familiar with. She performed as if she was a professional bartender and topped it off with a garnish of a lime twist.

We sat across the table from each other. I held up my glass and said, "To Winnie. May she find the strength to endure whatever lies ahead."

Carl said, "To Winnie. God bless our work mom." We clinked glasses.

Chatting until the early morning hours, I discovered Carl and I had more in common than I had realized. I learned that her breakup with her ex was similar to mine in that it was unexpected, and our exes weren't who we initially thought they were. The difference was that Carl's ex-boyfriend had been unfaithful, while my ex-fiancé was a full-blown hypocrite.

Another shared interest was that we both had an insatiable need to read and had stacks of books waiting to fulfill those desires, probably escapism on both our parts. In a close race with our love of books was our love of Broadway musicals. While I'd never been to New York, I'd seen performances when shows had travelled through Pittsburgh as well as local theater productions. Carl's excitement rose ten times when she talked about her experiences in New York City.

We agreed to save up to travel there and see as many shows as we could afford. She particularly wanted to see the musical *Mamma Mia* since ABBA was one of her grandmother's favorite groups. Carl shared heartwarming memories of her and her grandmother baking with the sounds of ABBA's album accompanying them. She said they made paper crowns and danced around her grandmother's house to the song "Dancing Queen."

We also shared a love of animals, particularly dogs. My heart ached when she told me that when they had parted ways, Michael had taken Ralph, their beloved basset hound. She fought to get him back, but since Michael had paid for the dog and had access to expensive lawyers, she had ultimately lost the fight. She showed me pictures on her phone of Ralph—many, many pictures. I told her about The Beast, and she happily agreed to join me when I next visited the shelter.

Carl was much wiser than I had originally given her credit. Feeling this connection with her was quite unexpected. She was an empathetic listener and seemed to have experienced more than her earthly twenty-two years. Her kindness and compassion caused a tiny fissure to form on my defensive shell and with the wine loosening my inhibitions, I felt a compelling need to unload the burden of the specifics of my incidents at Zelda's. *Will Carl be understanding and not judge me?*

Memories of those episodes hovered near the edge of my thoughts tempting me to release the bothersome details which had crept onto my lips nearly escaping. Luckily, fear of embarrassment overtook that brief lapse in judgment, and I quickly nixed the idea of revealing Lilloise to anyone.

Chapter Seven

Spring Creek 2011

It had been a little over a week since the second incident at Zelda's. I had gotten better at arriving to work on time even though I detoured several streets to avoid passing by the Weary Traveler's Antique Treasures. The switch to home brewed coffee contributed to my promptness, and the bonus was that I escaped the exorbitant cost of my caffeine fix from the Coffee Coffee Coffee House. Life seemed to go back to normal, mundane but my normal.

Winnie's husband went from the hospital to a rehab facility where he begged her to take him home. In order to fulfill his wish, she reached an agreement with Attorney Gladman. She worked at the office for four hours each morning while a home health nurse assisted Jim. The firm agreed that she could complete her remaining work duties from home. Arriving at the office two hours before everyone so that she could work undisturbed and leaving a few hours after our workday started left no time for us to socialize with her. I had not been thrilled with my position at the firm, but minus Winnie, I loathed it.

Mr. Avery was not happy with the arrangement, however since Mr. Gladman was the senior partner, there was not much cranky Mr. Avery could do. Winnie's absence from the office empowered Jessica even more as Winnie had always been our buffer. I avoided her by pretending to be on the phone when she passed by my cubicle or by sometimes hiding out in the restroom. Carl pinged my phone to warn me when Jessica was headed my way, and I returned the favor.

I worried that Winnie had taken on too much. Dark circles took up residence under her eyes. It was apparent she had lost a considerable amount of weight. She looked a lot like a small child playing dress up with adult clothing.

I stopped by her desk as she was about to leave. "Winnie, isn't there anything I can do to take some of your stress away?"

"You and Carl have done quite enough bringing us groceries and running errands for us. Your support has been more than we could ask for. It's in times of crisis that you realize who your friends really are."

I was touched that she had referred to me as a friend. "I'd like to do more, though. Is there anything else you might need?"

"If you don't have plans for dinner, will you and Carl join us tonight?"

"How will that help? You have enough to do without entertaining guests."

"We have so many people helping us from our church friends to Jim's pals, to my two lovely work friends. But everyone's lives are busy with their own families, and so they can only briefly stop by so that I can run errands. They bring us necessities, send cards, and support us in any way they can. But Jim and I are craving comradery and lengthier visits, not quick stop-by ones." She winked. "Besides, you two are not guests. You're like family to Jim and me."

I swallowed the lump that had begun to form. "We want to help, but not intrude."

"That's just it. We'd love it if someone would spend an entire evening with us. I don't mean to sound ungrateful for all that everyone has done to support us, but it's the simplest thing of connection that we crave. Jim especially needs connecting to the outside world. I think he's grown tired of my company and would like some variety of conversation."

"That's such a simple request. I'd be honored to spend the evening with you. My dinner plan was to pick up wonton soup and fried rice and probably eat alone while watching a game show on TV." After I said that, I realized how pathetic my life sounded.

"No takeout tonight! I'll be glad to cook for you." Winnie smiled.

I had not seen that smile in so long. It was comforting. I returned her smile.

I knocked on Winnie and Jim's front door with a bunch of white daisies and bright yellow sunflowers that looked like sunbursts. Flowers always cheered me, and my hope was that the bouquet would do the same for her.

Winnie answered the door. Her hair was neatly curled, and I spied a hint of makeup refreshing her face. "You are a dear." Winnie took the flowers, closed her eyes, and inhaled their scent. Then she kissed me on both cheeks.

"These chocolate-covered strawberries are for Jim." I handed her the box.

"You will be Jim's best friend with those chocolates. I've had him on a strict healthy diet. But I'll let him splurge tonight."

"Well, technically they are fruit." We both laughed. "I'm sorry Carl couldn't join us since she already had plans. But I'm glad to have both of you all to myself."

Winnie sighed. "She's been awfully closed mouth, but I suspect she's dating a new guy. I hope this one treats her well."

I nodded remembering the conversation Carl and I'd had comparing notes regarding loser boyfriends. However, Carl reminded me that we had come out of those relationships stronger and much wiser.

"Can I help in the kitchen?" Memories of Sully and I working side-by-side in his kitchen brought me the same peacefulness I'd felt when I had peeled, chopped, and stirred next to him.

"Absolutely not. That's my domain in this house. Jim is in the living room. Why don't you go and keep him company and I'll be in shortly with some hors d'oeuvres."

Before I entered the living room, I pasted on my biggest smile. Each time I saw Jim, I couldn't help but see Sully. As much as I prepared myself, I couldn't help being pulled back into the surf by the ocean's grief-ridden undertow. *You can do this, Jade...for Jim and for Winnie.*

Jim was in his wheelchair. On top of the table next to him was a bookstand displaying an opened book. I assumed Winnie had rigged that up so that Jim could turn the page without too much trouble.

"What are you reading?"

He pointed to the book on the stand, *Fall of Giants* by Ken Follett.

I was lucky to have been the first to borrow a copy from the library and had read nearly 1,000 pages in less than a week. Jim seemed to be about a quarter of the way through.

We went on to have an in-depth discussion about the novel and I discovered that Jim's interest also included WWII historical fiction as well as non-fiction. During our chat, Jim took his time forming sentences but occasionally slurred a few words—the same struggle as Sully had had. However, most of the time, I was able

61

to understand him, and he didn't seem to mind repeating if I needed him to. I admired the strength Jim showed when he could have easily felt sorry for himself. Sully had those same qualities.

My chest tightened as thoughts of Sully relentlessly pounded me like waves crashing on shore. I could not easily dismiss the thoughts of Sully and could not hold the waves of grief at bay. "I'll be right back. I'm going to see if Winnie needs some help in the kitchen."

I had just finished my sentence when Winnie entered with some stuffed grape leaves and an assortment of candied nuts. She and Jim threw some fun quips back and forth at each other giving me time to compose myself. She then announced that dinner would be in ten minutes and asked if I could escort Jim into the kitchen in a few. We were going to have dinner in the kitchen as Winnie had converted her dining room into Jim's bedroom since the stairs to the bedrooms were impossible for him to navigate.

Jim asked, "Can you wheel me into the kitchen? I only have strength in this one arm, so if I try to maneuver, I just go around in a circle." He laughed a deep belly laugh. I joined his laughter. I was amazed at how he had not lost his sense of humor.

The evening had started out as a spiritual boost for Winnie and Jim, but I think by the end of our time together, I was on the receiving end as well.

Chapter Eight

Spring Creek 2011

Carl and I got together and cooked in her elegant kitchen constructing meals for Winnie to have for a few days. Our time together in the kitchen reminded me of my dad and the times I had spent working in the kitchen with him.

"Can you peel these carrots?" Carl handed me a bag. I smiled.

"Carrots make you smile?" she asked.

"No. They just remind me of my dad. We cooked together and peeling carrots was my job." I lined up five carrots in formation on the cutting board and chopped the ends. "We used to call ourselves The Kitchen Ninjas." I surprised myself as I didn't usually talk about him so easily.

"Used to?" Carl questioned.

"He passed away a few months ago," I said. My voice cracked slightly.

"I'm so sorry." Carl placed her hand on my shoulder. "I didn't know."

"Not your fault. I rarely talk about him."

"I don't remember you going back to Pittsburgh for the funeral."

"That's where my mom and stepdad live. It was my biological dad, Sully, who had died." I stuttered at the word "died." That word seemed more permanent than saying passed away.

Carl's forehead scrunched as she was probably trying to understand my complicated family.

"Oh. So, was Sully from around here?" Her forehead remained unrelaxed.

"Not originally. But he spent about the last twelve years here in Spring Creek." I realigned the carrots.

"At least you had nearly thirty years with him." She nodded.

"Actually, only three years." That time my voice fully cracked.

"I'm confused." Hands on hips joined her scrunched forehead.

"My mom led me to believe that Thomas, my stepdad, was my biological dad."

And her original lie created so many ripples which caused deep wounds instead of supporting and protecting me.

"Hmmm." Carl returned me to the present. She nodded as if she was analyzing a complicated chart while trying to make sense of it.

"My mother never intended to tell me, but let it slip during an argument with me. However, she would not give me any details except his name, so I did one of those DNA tests and found a confirmed match to a man here in Spring Creek, Abraham Sullivan. Everyone called him Sully."

"Oh. I watched a TV show where this guy took like a DNA test, and he found out he had two other brothers and they'd been looking for him. He was a teacher and so were his brothers. They had all played football in different colleges, and each were married, and each had two daughters. It was a wild story. When they all met there were tears shed all over. I love those shows. They always make me cry. I sit with a box of tissues, cause I know I'll be a blubbering mess."

"Stay with me here, Carl."

"Sorry." Carl put a finger to her lips.

"So, I contacted him, and he was delighted to meet me. Turns out he never knew I existed. I moved here, found an apartment, and got a job at the law firm."

Carl leaned in cupping her cheeks in her palms.

My voice quivered at the memory, "We instantly became family."

"Did he have a wife and kids? What did they think of you?"

"He'd married but his wife had passed away several years before I met him. And they didn't have any children. He had said that I was a gift from heaven. But actually, he was a gift when I desperately needed one. I didn't get to keep my gift for very long, but I do get to hang on to the few memories we'd made."

It seemed easy to share with Carl. She nodded as if she understood my hurt and smiled when my story appeared to touch her heart.

"Sully and I spent as much time together as possible. It was wonderful until he had a series of strokes."

"Oh no," Carl's muffled words escaped through her hand covering her mouth.

"Much like Jim, Sully's stroke weakened his strength on one side. But his health deteriorated quickly. He spent the last few months of his life in a nursing facility. I went there every day and got to know the nurses very well. They were so kind and treated my dad well."

Tears filled Carl's eyes. "That stinks big time. You must miss him terribly."

I swallowed and blinked away the tears that had begun to form. "Sometimes, the memories bring me peace, but other times carrying the weight of it feels as if it will crush me at any moment. Reading about death and grief in novels, did not prepare me for the real thing. Those authors were good, but none could ever come close to describing the sorrow that enveloped my whole being. We were just beginning to build a relationship, and then I lost him."

"I'm so sorry, Jade. I wish I could have been there for you when all that was happening." She gave my shoulders a squeeze. "But I'm here now and if you ever need anything…"

"Thanks. I really appreciate your support especially since I've mostly kept to myself." I looked down at my hands clenched in my lap. "It's just that I have so many unanswered questions."

"Does he have any brothers or sisters who could give you answers?"

"No. He was an only child, and I've never met his parents, my grandparents, in person." I stared at the carrots looking like little soldiers. A flood of memories returned.

"Where are his parents, and why didn't they visit when he was sick?"

"They live in England, and Sully's father is extremely ill and can't travel. Sully's mother oversees her husband's care and therefore, couldn't leave him."

"Wow." Carl sighed.

"Sometimes, life can be so unkind."

"My past isn't so great, either. I try not to dwell in it, though." Carl stared out the window above the sink.

"If my future is anything like my past, then I'm doomed." Tears filled my eyes ready to spill over. My voice trembled, having to admit aloud, "I've a mother and stepdad whom I'm estranged from, and I have nothing in common with my half-brother." I couldn't believe I was spilling everything to her.

"You can always create a family with people who you choose. Lots of folks live miles from their families and create loving support from people physically nearer."

"Also, I've had a string of loser boyfriends including one wrenching heartbreak. I've not one long-term friendship, so how do I build a family from that? Not to mention, I'm in a job I detest, a town and an apartment too small to breathe in, and above all I was robbed of a father who loved me unconditionally for only three short years."

Carl shook her head, "Tch, tch, tch. Sounds like you've let lots of unhealthy thoughts take up permanent residence in your head." A lack of empathy oozing from her voice.

"I don't welcome them, but things just happen to me." I looked away from her accusatory stare.

"Some things may be out of our control, but many more are about how we handle experiences and ultimately the choices we make." Carl chuckled. "I think Winnie is rubbing off on me." She nodded, seeming proud of her growth. "There's not some godlike being playing a chess game with our lives making things just happen."

I resented her words even though deep down I feared there might be a little truth to them. My brain stalled and couldn't produce a counter response. She proved to be much, much wiser than my initial judgment of her being a bar hopper looking for the next inconsequential relationship.

"Come on. Let's finish this dinner and get it to Winnie and Jim before they starve. Then we can come back here and continue this deep dive into our souls." Carl winked.

On the drive to Winnie's, I thought about death and loss and how it seemed to unbalance my life. My grief in losing Sully was like an ocean swell. I'd be overcome one moment and then I'd remember a good memory and peace would still my mind. Maybe just having brief but beautiful memories was all I could really expect.

"Look at that sunset. It's as if Cézanne painted that landscape in this very sky." Carl pointed to the layers of pinks, magentas, oranges, and yellows. "Some people interpret that as a warning that darkness approaches. But to me, the beautiful colors predict a hopeful new day in my future. It's kind of a metaphor for life. You can dread the imminent darkness or get excited because potential adventures lie ahead. Your choice." Her outlook on life seemed so natural.

"I see your point, but it's not always easy just choosing to see things all unicorns and rainbows." I took another glance at the sunset trying to absorb her positivity.

"You're still mourning your father's death and focusing on the short time you had with him. Maybe in time that will fade, and you'll be able to be grateful for the divine time, as short as it was, that you had together."

I grimaced, not sure if I was willing to let go of my resentment and be ready to move on.

Carl shrugged, "Then maybe you can begin to heal and see your life as a blessing and not a tragedy. You can choose to move ahead and make choices your father would be proud of."

Those words hit me like an unexpected gut punch. My brain stalled, and once again she left me with nothing to say. Her words 'your father would be proud' immobilized me. I wondered if Sully would be proud of me.

After a while, the silence between us was deafening. I tried my hardest to come up with a counterpoint, but I could not. A young twenty-two-year-old gave me much to ponder. *Could it be that I was a cold hard pessimist?* I'd always thought of myself as a realist, but maybe I'd been fooling myself all along—a typical Jade Fair defense technique.

As if on cue, my negative nature interrupted any progress, albeit brief, I had made. "Yeah, yeah, yeah." I rolled my eyes. "Live every day like it's your last."

Carl glanced my way.

I tilted my head. "If it were my last day on Earth, I surely would not spend it at work. If I lived that mantra, I'd never go to work, I'd get fired, I wouldn't be able to pay my bills, I wouldn't be able to buy groceries. I'd eventually die." I was ready to go on with a long list of how that ridiculous phrase always made me cringe when Carl interrupted.

"I agree," Carl said.

Optimistic Carl agreed? I was stunned.

"You're right. We can't realistically live like that. But…"

"Oh yeah, here it comes, the but." I sighed.

It was Carl's turn to roll her eyes. "You can live each day like you just got another chance to get it right, to do the right thing, to make mistakes, to figure it out. And that, my dear friend, is the gift."

The silence lasted all the way to Winnie's house. Carl pulled into an empty spot a few doors away and ended the quiet, "Have you ever been in that antique store on Main Street?"

She shook me from my thoughts. I was relieved that she had changed the subject but quite startled that it was about Zelda's store. I stuttered, "Uh, uh, briefly, yes very briefly, once, maybe twice." I shifted in my seat. "Why do you ask?"

"I met this guy, Phoenix, at Garvey's Tavern and Brewhouse over in Embersville a couple of months ago. He's a drummer in the band, Mad Velvet Haze. We go out when he's in town and we FaceTime when he's not."

"I don't remember you ever mentioning him." I studied her face for clues as to why she's kept him a secret.

"I hadn't mentioned him because I didn't know if the relationship had potential or not."

In the six months since I'd known her, none of her so-called relationships had potential. That had never stopped her from sharing before. She must have really hoped that her connection with Phoenix would succeed and most likely did not want to jinx it. She probably hesitated to tell us, especially Winnie, because she did not want us judging her and offering our opinions.

I wondered what her dating had to do with Zelda's shop. Faking nonchalance, I asked, "So, what does Phoenix have to do with an antique shop?"

"He's really into pocket watches, and his birthday is in a few weeks. He'll be in town and we're going to celebrate." Carl engaged the car's turn signal as we approached the street where Winnie lived. "I thought maybe you'd know if they have jewelry and watches or is it just furniture?"

"She has all sorts of things from knickknacks to furniture." I tried to contain the nervousness in my voice. "I'm sure she has watches, too."

"She? Do you know the owner?"

"I've met her once or twice." I grimaced at the thought of Zelda.

"Would you mind going with me?" Carl's voice raised an excited octave. "I could use a negotiator."

I did not reply. My chest felt as if it was being squeezed in a vice when I entertained the thought of interacting with Zelda again. The last two instances sputtered through my mind. I shuddered when I recalled how she had put me under her spell.

"I'm sorry. I put you on the spot." Carl steered her car into a free space in front of Winnie's house. "I can go by myself."

"No. I'd be glad to go with you," I lied. "I'm not much of a negotiator, but I can offer moral support." My words were the opposite of my thoughts. Maybe I could use Carl as a shield so that Zelda's mysterious influence could not affect me.

Chapter Nine

Spring Creek 2011

Returning to the scene of the crime was not as bad as I had anticipated. Probably because I had Carl's illusory protection. Still, it gave me some comfort even if it was based on an artificial sense of security created in my mind. When we entered the shop, Zelda ran to me and embraced me as if I were a lost puppy.

"Jade Fair! I've missed you," she planted a kiss on each cheek.

Carl glanced sideways at me. Probably because I had implied that I barely knew Zelda. I shrugged off her look. "Zelda, this is my friend, Carl."

Zelda embraced Carl as if they had been lifelong friends. I could tell she was immediately smitten by Zelda's exuberance. When Carl explained that she was there for a pocket watch, Zelda was as excited to flaunt the watches as she had been when she first introduced me to the snow globes.

I stuck by Carl as if we were conjoined—an assurance I had hoped would prevent handling a snow globe and avoid an unwanted incident. Carl decided on a small brass pocket watch etched with a fleur-de-lis on one side. She and Zelda agreed on a price. It seemed an expensive gift for someone Carl had only known a short time, however she did not solicit my opinion, so I kept my thoughts to myself.

The only thing left was for the transaction to be completed with a piece of rectangular plastic. I thought I was home free until Carl said, "Oops, I left my purse in the car." Faster than a gazelle, she was out the door. "I'll be right back," she called from the sidewalk.

Fear traveled from my hair follicles to the tips of my toes. I did not want to be alone with Zelda even for the briefest of moments. When Zelda disappeared into another room, I startled myself with an unrecognizable sigh—a combination of relief and trepidation.

Hurry up, Carl. Hurry. Please hurry. My silent pleas were dashed when Zelda returned with another snow globe. It contained the miniature Louvre but was quite different from the others. This one, a bit larger and not as ornate as the smaller version, piqued my interest. However, my curiosity to learn more about Lilloise was outweighed by the fear of being under Zelda's spell. I thrust my hands into my pockets. I was sure I had outwitted her this time.

"Look at this one, Jade Fair." Zelda tipped the globe so that the snow at the bottom stirred like a funnel-shaped waterspout. "Another one from mystical Paris."

You're the mystical one, not Paris.

"I noticed the majority of the snow globes are from Paris." I made sure my hands were still hidden in the depths of my pockets. "Any idea why?"

"That's something to ponder, isn't it Jade?" She smiled and stretched her arm toward me, globe in hand.

I grasped at the fabric in the bottom of my pockets to ensure my hands resisted any unwanted object placement. The bell above the door rang, and in skipped Carl waving a credit card as if she were parading a flag after a strategic battle win. Zelda placed the globe onto a table next to me. I was finally able to exhale. Carl paid, we exited the store, and I sprinted toward the car.

"Hey! Wait up, Jade," Carl yelled. "What's the rush?"

I attempted to come up with a plausible reason. "I don't want you to get a ticket in case the meter ran out." I called over my shoulder. It was a flimsy fib, but I thought she might buy it.

"They don't issue tickets after six o'clock." She caught up to me. "You didn't know that?"

I fibbed again, "I forgot."

Carl shook her head, suggesting she did not believe me. She drove me the few short blocks to my apartment. "Thanks for introducing me to Zelda. Her store is amazing and so is she." Carl hugged her purchase to her heart. "Phoenix is going to love this."

I hoped her relationship with Phoenix was going to succeed. She deserved that. My wish was for her to be able to have a relationship like Winnie and Jim. I admired their relationship.

They were dedicated to each other in ways I'd never experienced nor witnessed. Each had individual interests, and each had strengths that supported the other.

The possibility of a commitment with a guy who was honest, trustworthy, and not a prejudiced jerk would have been a welcomed change. If I had ever gotten an opportunity to develop a serious relationship with someone as kind as Jim, my life would have turned out so much better. Ironically, it was a dog that gave me a glimpse of the companionship I needed. The Beast was loyal and would not desert me.

The next Sunday, Carl and I worked again in her kitchen constructing a tray of lasagna (Jim's favorite), a pot of beef vegetable soup (Winnie's favorite), and seafood stew (my favorite recipe from Sully.) Carl needed to get ready for her dinner date with Phoenix, so when we finished, I took the food to Winnie and Jim's house.

Winnie met me on the sidewalk. "I'll help you into the house with these, but then do you mind if I run to the pharmacy?" She reached into the trunk of my car for one of the boxes. "They close early on Sundays."

"Go now or you'll never make it in time." I took the box from her. "I'll stay with Jim."

Winnie thanked me and raced to her car. It took me three trips, but I got all the food into the kitchen. The soup, stew, and some side dishes went into the refrigerator, I placed the lasagna into the oven on low to keep it warm, and then got out plates, utensils, and glasses to set the table.

"Winnie," Jim called from the living room. "Winnie," he called again.

I walked to the doorway. "Winnie had to run to the pharmacy. She'll be back shortly."

Jim sat in a recliner propped up with pillows. He had on black dress pants, a crisply ironed baby blue shirt, and a matching blue and white striped tie. He and Winnie watched church services on their television from home on Sundays and Winnie made sure they dressed as if they were there in person. That's just like Winnie to ensure Jim's stroke affected their lives in the least way possible.

"Oh. Hi Jade." Jim grinned a lopsided smile. The stroke had affected the left side of his face, arm, and leg. "Is it your turn to babysit me?" He had maintained his sense of humor.

"Heavens no." I sat on the couch next to him. "It's my turn to have the privilege of your company." I reached over and patted his hand. His cool skin took me straight to the memory of the hours I spent holding my dad's hand when he was in the hospital and then the nursing home.

Jim stroked the back of my hand with his right hand. "Winnie's really lucky to have you girls in her life." He spoke slowly and slurred a few of the words. "I'm lucky by way of association."

I loved the sincerity of his words. I countered, "I think we're the lucky ones to be able to call you and Winnie our friends."

"Your friendship means a lot, but you've become more like family to us." A rogue tear escaped and slid to his chin. "Winnie thinks of you girls as her daughters."

I dabbed his cheek and chin with a tissue. *Perhaps there was some truth to Carl's beliefs. Maybe, just maybe, family can be more than just the people with whom I was related.*

Jim continued, "You filled the void in our lives since Jenny and her girls and our other daughter, Crystal live so far away."

A lump formed in my throat. I quickly changed the subject. "I brought your favorite, lasagna. I'd better go check on it, so it doesn't dry out."

"I have a new favorite." Jim chuckled. "That seafood stew you brought last week. I hope there's some of that, too."

"Yep! That happens to be my favorite, also." We fist bumped.

"You have some mean recipes with some distinctive variations on standard techniques. Ever think of cooking professionally?"

"I can't take all the credit. Most of the unique recipes are ones I had inherited from my father."

"Well, thank him for me."

I just smiled. I didn't want to ruin Jim's mood by revealing that Sully was no longer with us.

I was surprised Jim did not know. I had assumed that Winnie had told him, but maybe he had forgotten, or quite possibly the stroke not only affected him physically, but also compromised his memory.

Chapter Ten

Spring Creek 2011

I leaned onto Carl's neat and orderly desk. She had a framed picture of a group of people dressed alike on a beach at sunset. In the photo on Carl's lap sat two children identical in looks to each other and hair that mimicked Carl's dark tresses minus the blue. I supposed they were the nieces she spoke of so often. *That would be so nice to have a family to vacation with.*

"I need your help." I whispered.

"Why are you whispering?" Carl asked.

I nodded my head toward Jessica who strode by the cubical like the tortoise in the infamous race. She tucked her hair behind her ears. *The better to hear you with!* The words echoed in my head. I rolled my eyes.

Carl mimed "text me.".

I nodded and returned to the safety of my cubicle and messaged Carl.

Brother texted. Mom in car accident.

Shit! She hurt?

Not conscious

Yikes! When did that happen?

A few days ago.

You just finding out?

He didn't contact me until she was stable.

Carl texted an image of a woman slapping her forehead.

Going home?

???

Talk at lunch

Okay

After discussing my options with Carl, she convinced me that I should go home even though I hadn't spoken to my mother and stepfather in years. My relationship with my half-brother was strained, but not nonexistent and he might need my support.

Compassionate Mr. Gladman said to take all the time I needed. While I appreciated his kindness, I told him I did not plan on being gone long.

I loaded the car and began the six-hour drive to Pittsburgh. I thought about Carl's words describing families not only as lineage by birth but created with people we choose to surround ourselves with through love. I realized I was not grounded by family anywhere. I did not consider Spring Creek home, but neither did I consider Pittsburgh home anymore.

I also thought a lot about Winnie and the relationship she had with Jim as well as the tight friendships she had with her church ladies and volunteer organizations. I had that missing in my life—connections. I searched my heart and brain as to why and decided to heed Sully's words and leave the past behind and focus on the bonds I had been forging with Winnie, Jim, and Carl. It was a start which was huge for me.

I took a bite of the peanut butter sandwich I'd brought with me and washed it down with a big gulp of coffee that had gone cold.

In the silence of the drive, negative thoughts crept in, and I thought about how past failures had paralyzed me. Winnie had told me that I made decisions based on fear of being rejected. I contemplated her words and then attempted to stop the negative stream by shouting, "It serves no purpose." I turned on the radio to help drown out those thoughts.

I sang along with Bruno Mars' *Just the Way You Are*, made up words if I didn't know them, and then laughed at myself because sometimes my version did not make sense at all.

When Coldplay's song, *Paradise* came on the radio, it sent my imagination whirling as to what Paradise would look like for me. It was quite the opposite of Spring Creek.

Then the Kelly Clarkson song, *Because of You,* played next. The lyrics seared through my heart with a sharpness that no amount of tears could wash away. It was as if Ms. Clarkson had fully examined the painful relationship I had endured with my mother and concluded she had an unnatural detachment toward me. That mother-daughter relationship was one of the main sources which had caused me to mistrust others.

At hour four, I found myself emotionally drained by all the reminiscing. After several attempts at finding a clear signal, the radio stations produced only static or indecipherable sounds. I gave up and switched it off. The silence was a welcome relief until my thoughts started spiraling again.

I searched for another radio station and finally found a clear signal, Adele was part way through the song, *Rolling in the Deep.* I couldn't catch a break as those words repeated the searing of my heart, but this time returned me to thoughts of Nicholas and our breakup. It was too painful to listen to, so I searched a few other stations and found either static again or nothing comforting. I turned the radio off. Silence seemed better than torturous reminders of the past.

Alone again with only my thoughts, I pondered if I should return to college and finish my degree, or just try to find a better paying job or one that at the very least had better benefits.

I needed a break to stretch my legs, so I pulled into a rest stop and decided to call Carl. Since it was after the law firm's business hours, I called her cell. I normally would rely on Winnie for advice, but she was consumed with Jim's care. Carl answered on the first ring.

"Hey, girl! How's the drive going?" she asked.

How do I summarize hours of thoughts and contemplations about my life and things that have happened to me which placed this thirty-year-old in a confused state in life? It was like being stuck in a roundabout with no exits.

"Jade. Are you there?"

"Yes. You asked how the drive was going." I unbuckled my seatbelt. "I'm about four hours in and it feels like forty."

"I've just arrived at Winnie's." Carl's voice muffled, "I'm staying with Jim so she can go to her eye appointment."

"Call me later?" I tried not to sound disappointed.

"Sure thing. Bye." Carl ended the call.

Not wanting to be alone with my thoughts again, I called Will next. His assistant answered. "William Fair's office. How may I help you?" She sounded like she was twelve years old.

"Is Mr. Fair available?" I attempted to sound formal like it was a business call.

"I'm sorry. He's currently in a meeting. May I take a message?"

"Thank you, no. I'll try back later." I hung up before she could convince me otherwise.

After a short break, I resumed driving. However, the silence in the car started my brain running through my past again. Will and I were never very close partly because he was five years younger, but mostly because we were so opposite. He excelled in sports, had numerous friends, and was valedictorian of his high school class.

On the other hand, I connected with characters in novels, fantasized about a romantic life, and was accepted into my last choice of colleges, which I attended but did not complete a degree.

At twenty-five, Will already had a successful career in the real estate business. An apprenticeship fell into his lap his last year of college, and he had secured a position in one of Pittsburgh's top companies even before he had graduated. They had paid his tuition to obtain an MBA from Carnegie Mellon, of course. I was never jealous because that was not a path I had wanted. I was, however, envious of all the opportunities that had just materialized for him. I thought about how my life would have been so different if I'd had the same breaks as Will.

There was a lifetime to think about during those six hours. Some memories produced tears and some even a few smiles. My thoughts returned to Carl's suggestion of surrounding myself with people I love and trust. That was going to be difficult since that would require me to open myself up to possible rejection and hurt. But I admired Winnie's commitment toward others and Carl's enthusiasm toward life. I longed for the kind of friendship I had once had with Tiffany all those years ago. Even after all that time, my heart was still warmed by thoughts of her. I knew that she had not abandoned me, circumstances had, but it still hurt years later.

Thoughts of Tiffany naturally migrated to Lilloise. Logic told me that Lilloise was nonexistent akin to characters in novels, but I felt as if we could have been friends. I would have liked to have gotten to know her and Marguerite. I wondered what had happened to their friendship. I also wondered about Lilloise's father. What had caused him to go from the soft-spoken, seemingly loving father to a gruff, impatient one during my second snow globe experience into their past? I knew the only way to find answers to those questions was to visit Zelda and take a third questionable journey. But that thought left me gasping for breath.

I pushed aside those scary thoughts which surprisingly morphed into an unexplainable exhilaration. It was extremely ridiculous to entertain the thought of traveling back in time again and even worse, letting it excite me.

Could it have possibly been that I wanted to know more about Lilloise and Marguerite's friendship to learn if they had ever reunited unlike Tiffany and me? However, Lilloise and Marguerite seemed to have a unique deeper connection. I concluded that it must have been the caffeine energizing me and perpetuating bizarre thoughts of time travel being real.

At hour five, it was time to stop for another essential coffee refill and most importantly a much-needed bathroom break. I also wanted to give my brain a respite from all the reminiscing.

An employee swept past obviously at the end of her shift and pointed to a co-worker and said, "I'll see you tomorrow." She'd emphasized each word exactly like I had said to Sully after each visit in the nursing home. I had wanted to make sure that he knew he was not alone, and that I would always be there for him. He would nod and respond in a whisper, "I'll see you tomorrow." He'd wink, point back at me, and flash the biggest smile his weak muscles could muster.

Until that one Thursday. I had been excited to share some news about our favorite author coming out with another novel. We had a lovely conversation. Mostly me doing the talking because at that point Dad had struggled to get enough breath to complete a sentence. I had told him about some new recipes I had wanted to try, and then I shared some gossip from work which I might have exaggerated a bit just to see him smile.

After chatting, I read to him a few chapters of *Mozart's Last Aria* by Matt Rees until it was apparent that Sully was fighting to keep his eyes open so that he could spend as much time with me as possible. I kissed him on each cheek and then paused in the doorway as I did each evening before leaving. I pointed at him, and said, "I'll see you tomorrow." He smiled, nodded, and instead of pointing back at me, he pointed toward the ceiling. I blew him a kiss and had left him as usual. I dismissed the misplaced finger point as a mistake or perhaps he had not had the strength to lift his arm toward me. The next day, I realized he had been pointing toward heaven, because before morning, he was gone. I have hated Thursdays ever since.

Chapter Eleven

Shadyside, Pittsburgh PA 2011

I circled the city block three times before finding a parking spot and then maneuvered my Chevy into the parallel parking space with ease. Some things were simple to remember, other things I wished I could forget. The sounds and smells of Pittsburgh's Shadyside neighborhood transported me to my younger days. Not much had changed since I had last lived there.

My mouth watered as the aroma of freshly baked bread, black/white cookies, and the famous cinnamon rolls spilled onto the sidewalk from Rizen's Bakery. It was good to see the familiar stores. Sandwiched between Miller's Hardware and Angelo's Shoe Repair was The Whale Bookstore. I spent many hours perusing those shelves. I recalled Mr. Angelo and the distinct smell of leather which had permeated the air from his shop. Everyday walking to and from school, I'd see him sitting outside on a folding chair talking to whoever had stopped to chat. To me, he seemed old twenty years ago.

And there he was on the same chair. He waved when I'd driven by looking for a parking spot. Not because he remembered me, but more likely because he waved to everyone. He was Shadyside's one-man welcoming committee. Passing by The Peddler's Shoes and Things brought back memories of Thomas taking me for new school shoes each August before the new school year began. Mr. Shu would always side with me when Thomas would try to convince me of more practical shoes. I had to suppress a chuckle every time I said his name—Mr. Shu who owned a shoe store. He was one of my favorite people. He was so nice and kind to everyone.

I walked to the next block and there it sat on the corner of Alder and Myrtle Streets. The four-story red brick building that had housed my childhood. I still possessed the key to my mom and Thomas' apartment, but I did not think it appropriate to use since I had not communicated with them in so long. After a deep breath in to calm my nervousness, I pushed the button for apartment 206. The door buzzed. I gathered as much courage as possible and entered. Luckily, I had only packed for a few days, so my suitcase was not very heavy. I trudged up the first flight of stairs, stopping on the first landing in order to catch my breath. In my delusive world, I was in better shape and thought I could make it without pausing.

Thomas was at the top and hurried down the last few steps to grab my bag. "Let me help you there, Jade." I only caught a glimpse, but he looked as if he had aged quite a bit since I had last seen him.

"Thanks Dad." I'd considered addressing him as Thomas, but I had addressed him as Dad for twenty-seven years. Besides, he had raised me, went to all my recitals, and comforted me when Mom and I quarreled. I couldn't help but think of him as my dad even though I still harbored feelings of resentment that he had been complicit with Mom's secrets and lies.

"Will had told me you'd be here today, but he wasn't sure what time."

"I'm sorry. I should have called to let you know when I'd be arriving."

"No problem. I'm just glad you're here." He held the apartment door open for me. "How was the drive?"

"Long." I hung my purse on the coat rack and placed my jacket and hanging clothes across a living room chair, the same green paisley one, minus the plastic covering, which they had inherited from my grandmother. "But at least the weather cooperated." I examined his face, and it revealed signs of defeat. The wrinkles residing on his forehead were increasingly pronounced and the creases around his mouth sat like two deep parentheses.

"Your mother's anxious to see you." He turned away so I could not tell if he was sincere or not without the ability to connect his facial expression with his words.

A bit of necessary silence ensued. I filled the awkward silence by glancing around the apartment I had not seen in three years or more. Most of it remained the same as before I had left for Spring Creek. And before that, even when I had lived away at college for a stint not much had changed. After I had moved in with Nicholas, get-togethers with my parents and Will were usually at restaurants or at Will's place, so I felt as if I had not really been in that space for quite some time.

"I'll put your bag in your bedroom for you." Thomas headed down the hall. I followed.

It was odd feeling like a guest in a place where I had lived for eighteen years, but the photographs lining the hall walls indicated that at one time, I had been a resident here. There were several large eight by ten framed photos—one of me in my high school graduation gown and cap, one of Will in his, and also one of Will's university graduation.

I stopped at the one professional photo of the four of us that mom had insisted we participate in. Each one of us had a huge grin. Probably the photographer made us laugh by telling a joke. The memory of how she had gotten us to smile had faded, but it reminded me that when a camera is pointed toward people, they almost always smile, regardless of what is really going on in their lives. Those smiles had not represented what had really been going on with the Fair family.

Entering my bedroom was like a slap in the face. While I had not assumed that they would have kept it as a shrine to me, I did not expect it to be wiped clean of my existence. When I had last seen it, the general hue of the room had been pastel peach and muted seafoam green, the paint colors I had chosen. The wooden narrow-planked floors had been protected by a large area rug with the same colors, and even the bedspread and lampshades had matched the color palette.

The current state could only be described as white-washed…white walls, white curtains, white bedspread, and white rug. In the corner, where my bookshelf used to stand, now housed a table with my mother's sewing machine and accessories. Anything I had left behind when I had moved out, was nowhere to be seen.

Thomas must have felt my angst because he successfully interrupted my thoughts and the negative path I was about to go down. He cleared his throat, "How about a bit of dinner, and then we can head to the nursing home?" Despite his effort to sound lighthearted, there was understandable sadness in his tone.

I was not hungry due to the multitude of snacks I had consumed during the drive. However, I was not anxious for the inescapable mother-daughter reunion, therefore a delay was appreciated. I was only there under obligation to Will and Thomas. So, I forced a smile and said, "That sounds like a plan."

Dinner with him was not as uncomfortable as I had thought it would be. He did most of the talking. Mostly small talk. He avoided telling me the details of Mom's car accident because his voice cracked each time he tried. So, he proceeded with information about her stay in the hospital and her recovery the past few days in the rehabilitation facility. It only got awkward when he said, "We really miss you, Jade."

I had no response, and I am sure my silence conveyed to him a whole lot more than my unkind words would have.

I finally asked, "Is Will meeting us there?"

"He has yet another work engagement." Dad shifted in his chair. "He had said he'd try to get out of it."

By the tone of his voice and his uneasiness, I sensed there was more to it than "another work engagement."

After dinner, Dad cleared the table while I changed out of my coffee-stained blouse which also appeared as if I'd slept in it. We were mostly silent during the twenty-minute drive to Mom's facility.

Dad entered Mom's room first. "Look who I found!" He forced excitement through his words instead of what probably should have been sarcasm.

I stepped out from behind him and got my first look at her. A slight gasp escaped through my lips. I tried to cover it up by coughing. She looked so small and frail in the wheelchair. This accident did more than break her leg and arm, it seemed to break her spirit, too. Will had not described the scene accurately at all. Or maybe I just dismissed him when he tried to warn me.

Vibrant, opinionated Evie had been reduced to a sad disheveled being. I gave her a gentle hug as if she was an ancient vase and would disintegrate at the slightest touch. I could feel several bones protruding from her bird-bone back. She had always had a slight build but was never that thin. Surely her frail condition could not have happened in the few days since the accident. I patted her uninjured hand acting like I wasn't shocked by her injuries. I could have won an Oscar for that performance.

Behind her left ear was a significant sized bandage. There were still signs of fresh cuts on her cheek, nose, and upper lip "I'm so sorry this happened to you." I swallowed away the burning in my throat. "Dad told me it was a drunk driver."

"I don't know. Was it, Thomas? I don't remember…anything about the accident." She looked down at the cast on her left arm. "Thomas said he'd told me what had happened when I was in the hospital, but I don't remember being there either." She shrugged.

"That's probably pretty typical when you've been through trauma." I attempted to console her even though she didn't seem bothered by her lack of memory.

Her attention during the conversation jumped to random thoughts not related to whatever we were discussing. While she talked about the color of her slippers, she looked me up and down and then said, "You're so pretty."

I backed away to get a better look at her facial expression to see if she was being sarcastic. I had never heard her utter those words or anything remotely like them when referring to me. I had overheard her say those words to my childhood friend, Tiffany, several times, but never to me.

She touched the cast on her arm gazing at it as if it was the first time she had seen it. She looked at me with eyes glazed with confusion. Then as if she snapped back to the present she repeated, "Hi! You're so pretty."

I knew she apparently was not wrapped in reality, so I said, "Thank you. So are you."

She brought her hand to her cheek as if embarrassed. I could not have predicted how her next words would affect me. She stared at me, briefly nodded, and then said, "You have the loveliest green eyes. Reminds me of your father."

I gasped at the air. Then my gasp was accompanied by the strangest sound.

Since Thomas had grey-blue eyes, she had to have been referring to Sully. Then she muddled my brain even more. "That's why I named you Jade."

I looked from her to Thomas and then back to her. She had always told me that she had named me Jade because that was her favorite stone. Shaken, I was at a loss as to what to do or say. Perspiration pooled on my forehead and above my lip. She had never mentioned Sully except during the argument when she had told me that Thomas was not my father. And even then, quite hesitantly, she had revealed only his first and last name.

And then in her brain stupor she said, "Did you feed Scruffy?" She pursed her lips. "He's your responsibility, you know."

Panicked at what had just transpired, I looked at Dad for help. Scruffy was a stray cat I had taken in shortly after Tiffany had moved to Texas. Mom had protested having a cat in her home, but Dad had convinced her that it would teach me responsibility. Dad's argument had been a guise; it was more like his attempt to cheer me. Scruffy was mangy looking but cute in his own disheveled way. He loved to be aloof and then when he desired, would cuddle, purr, and rub his face on my neck. He had definitely favored Mom, though. When she'd leave the apartment, he'd sit by the door staring at it as if telepathy would bring her back through the wooden structure separating them. The vet had estimated he was approximately twelve to fourteen years old when we took him in, and he had only lived a few more years. Mom tried to hide it, but she had cried more than any of us.

"Evie darling," Dad stroked her cheek. "Scruffy has been gone for years."

"I know that!" Mom chuckled, "I was just thinking about what a nice cat he was."

"He was the best." Dad validated her obvious coverup.

Her frailty caused me to stare, and I realized I harbored conflicting emotions which apparently had the ability to coexist. I made note to occasionally remind myself to never take that revelation for granted. Apparently, I could have empathy for someone who had hurt me so badly.

Mom's blonde tufts were like whirling dervishes desperately hanging onto graying roots. "Would you like me to fix your hair?" I offered. She would have been devastated for anyone to see her like that if she had been aware of its state.

"That would be lovely." She smiled and nodded.

I rummaged through my purse to find hair clips or anything that might help tame her unintended hairdo. I did not own a brush since brushes are villains for us curly-haired women. I found one in the drawer of her bedside table. Careful to avoid the bandage, I gently stroked through the confused matted mop.

With each stroke I was reminded of my childhood when she had attempted to brush my strong curls. Most times I had not allowed her comments to injure my spirit, but sometimes I had not been tough enough to ignore them, and her words struck deeper than a glacial crevasse. More than once she had said, "Your hair is so dry." And then she'd added, "You need to brush it at least three times a day and one hundred strokes every night." She had accused me of not using the hair products she'd purchased even though I told her that they didn't work on my hair. Her words had made me feel as if I had been at fault. Luckily, I didn't let her harsh words deter me, I eventually found products that were right for me, and I grew to love my curls.

"That feels so nice." She closed her eyes. "Maybe you could also paint my nails."

"It looks like someone has already painted them," I replied. "They're a lovely blue. Your favorite."

"They are pretty." She glanced down at her nails and stroked them like she was seeing them for the first time. "Who painted them?"

Thomas smiled. "I did." He took her hand, kissed it, and held it to his cheek. For all she had put him through, his enduring love for her could not have been more apparent.

"Thank you," she whispered. Tenderness reflected in her eyes. Something I had never witnessed.

We stayed barely an hour as our visit seemed too much stimulation for Mom. She became more confused and dozed off mid conversation. A worker came in to get her ready for bed, and so we said our goodbyes for the evening. I could not give voice to the familiar words 'I'll see you tomorrow.' So, I just said, "Bye, Mom."

On the ride home, Dad told me that she was on heavy-duty meds and often got confused. The doctors weren't concerned as it was typical behavior for a trauma patient in addition to the drugs' effects.

Back at the apartment, Dad offered to make me tea or something stronger, but I told him it was a long day, and I wanted to turn in early. He looked at the clock and just smiled. It was only a little before eight, but I was physically, mentally, and emotionally exhausted. Even after being alone with my thoughts on the long drive, I needed solitude, time to process, and to breathe. I kissed him on the forehead. He thanked me for coming. I detected a tone of repentance in his voice.

The anger I had held onto the past several years, seemed to be inconsequential at that moment. I was relieved at how the circumstances encouraged my resentment to dissipate. I prayed it would remain at bay.

Chapter Twelve

Shadyside, Pittsburgh PA 2011

The next morning, Thomas and I worked in the kitchen side by side. As we prepared breakfast, I smiled remembering similar moments with Sully. I had a momentary feeling of guilt as if Thomas would replace Sully's memory. Luckily that feeling quickly passed as a twinge of Carl's optimism surfaced. Instead, I realized I would never choose to have Thomas replace Sully's memory. And if I could be open to it, the possibility of Thomas widening my circle of support was within my power.

In contrast to the day before, his demeanor appeared more relaxed and the crevasses on his brow followed suit. The silence between us was peaceful and not at all uncomfortable. I supposed we were both enjoying each other's company. I wondered what he might have been thinking as my mind wandered to my high school yearbook which I had been looking through the past evening.

I broke the silence. "Yesterday, when I had hung my coat in the hall closet, I found my middle school yearbooks on one of the shelves. I had a good time going down memory lane." I chuckled. "I was a pretty dorky-looking middle schooler."

"Oh, my goodness!" He dropped the whisk and hurried from the kitchen.

Confused, I followed him into the living room. "What just happened?"

"I totally forgot to give you this note." He rifled through a stack of mail on an end table. "She was here two days ago." He handed me a used envelope with a phone number written on it.

"Whose phone number is this?" I turned the envelope over to see if there was any other information.

"Her name was Tiffany. Said she knew you in middle school." He rubbed his forehead with the back of his hand. "I'm so sorry I forgot to give this to you. She said she'd be in town for a couple of days."

"Tiffany was my best friend in sixth grade." My voice rose in pitch. "We'd lost touch. I tried to find her on the internet, but I had no luck. I'd assumed she'd married and changed her last name and that's why I couldn't locate her." I smiled at the thought that this scribbled phone number could be the means to being able to reconnect with her.

"Yes. I remember her now." Dad seemed as excited as me. "Call her. Call her. Maybe she's still in town."

I retrieved my cell from the bedroom, shakily entered the ten digits, and tapped the green circle. My heart thumped an uncontrollable rhythm as the call went through. It proceeded immediately to voicemail where I fashioned a pitiful message, "Hi

Tiffany. This is Jade. Jade Fair. I'm so happy to hear from you. Please call me at your convenience." *Please call me at your convenience. Why did I make it sound like a business call? I'm back to being that sixth-grade self-conscious nerd!*

Less than ten minutes later, my phone buzzed. The same number which I had entered, appeared on the screen. I answered, "Hello." One little word and we went right into a conversation as if we had never been separated.

She told me she had married, and her last name was Faison. She had become a surgeon as was her husband. She was in Pittsburgh interviewing for a position in the thoracic department at Allegheny General Hospital. She was not sure she and her husband were interested in relocating, but this was her specialty and was in Pittsburgh to see if it could be a fit. She was returning later that day to New Orleans, where she and her husband resided. So, we agreed to meet for lunch at Eat'n Park, which was our favorite middle school hangout. We had always laughed at the name because no one ever ate first and then parked their cars.

I was so excited, I arrived thirty minutes early. Tiffany arrived shortly thereafter. It was as if no time had elapsed between us. Conversation flowed so easily, we had to remind each other to take a breath.

"I've filled you in on the last sixteen, no seventeen…oh my! Has it been eighteen years?" She shook her head. "I can't believe it's been that long."

"So much has happened in those many years." I nodded.

"Catch me up on everything that's happened in your life since we've lost touch."

I sucked in a bunch of air. "Your life seems to have taken a clear path while mine has been like a dingy set out on open waters." I laughed to cover up my embarrassment.

"Oh, Jade." She tilted her head. "What happened to my optimistic friend?"

"Life happened. That's what." Tears swelled in my eyes. I laughed again to hustle them away. *Maybe I had been naively optimistic back then.*

"I know that eleven-year-old Jade is still in there just waiting patiently for you to discover her again and set her free." Tiffany squeezed my hand.

At that moment, with Tiffany's encouraging words, I felt as if I was eleven again and anything was possible. "As I told you on the phone, I'm in Pittsburgh because of my mom being in an accident."

"I'm so sorry about that." She grimaced. "Your dad had told me a few of the details when I had stopped by. I'm leaving today, but if there is anything, absolutely anything I can do, please don't hesitate to ask."

Her empathetic voice took me right back to middle school. No matter how bad my day was, I could always count on her to listen and understand. "She's banged up pretty badly, but the doctors are hoping for a full recovery. Thomas is by her side every day, and that is helpful."

"Wow. Life can change in an instant." She shook her head.

She had no idea, but I was about to let her in on a few of my life-changing "instants."

"You are so right about that." *Here goes.* "First of all, I learned several years ago that Thomas was not my biological dad."

Her bangs obstructed my view, but I was sure she had raised her eyebrows. "They kept that information from you?"

"That's a nice way to put it, but yes they'd lied." I went on to tell her the sordid details. It was so refreshing to have a friend who I could count on to not judge me, and yet she could still include her heartfelt opinion.

After several hours, Tiffany's husband, Marcellus, met us at the restaurant. Tiffany stood to greet him. He was so tall that he overshadowed Tiffany by at least a foot even though she was not a tiny lady. He sported a navy suit, a crisp white shirt, and a striped, pink tie. His braids neatly intertwined at the base of his neck completed his well-coiffed look. Tiffany and Marcellus were a beautiful couple inside and out. He kissed his wife on the cheek and hugged her as if he had not seen her in weeks. It warmed my heart to witness a marriage that was truly loving instead of an obligation as my mother's attitude toward Thomas had been.

Tiffany introduced me, "Marcellus, I'd like you to meet my very good friend, Jade."

I was touched that she still considered me to be a very good friend.

"It's my pleasure to meet you." He gently shook my hand. "Tiffany was so excited for this reunion." His soft voice complimented his handshake.

"Nice to meet you, too." I pointed to an empty chair. "Won't you join us?"

"I wish I could." He turned to Tiffany. "But if we're to make our flight, we need to be on our way."

My heart sank, but we departed both agreeing we would ardently keep in touch.

The meeting with Tiffany left me nostalgic for happier times in Pittsburgh. So, I drove to the base of the Duquesne Incline, parked, and rode the incline to the top. I strolled along Grandview Avenue stopping at the lookout platform to observe the city. It continued to be my favorite view of the skyline.

Following my high school graduation, my family and I had come here to take pictures of me in my cap and gown with the city scape in the background. People had stopped and stared at us causing my self-consciousness to rise. And then a few people had clapped and shouted congratulatory greetings, which then caused me to be thoroughly embarrassed. However, the best part was when my parents surprised me and treated the four of us to a fancy celebration luncheon at The LeMont Restaurant. I really did have some memorable times in the city.

The clock on the nightstand next to my childhood bed glared at me. It illuminated two a.m. as if to mock me. I longed for sleep, but it evaded me. I kept going over my meeting with Tiffany, how I craved for the friendship we once had, and why for all those years since, I had been unable to attain another. With all that had happened in the past week, I had mostly pushed aside thoughts of Lilloise and Marguerite as well as Zelda's trances.

Recalling the day Tiffany had moved to Texas evoked images of Lilloise and Marguerite's heart-wrenching scene. I wondered about the two women, if they ever got to see each other again, and what became of Lilloise's relationship with her father.

Was it stupid of me to want to travel there again? The desire was there, but fear had once again paralyzed me from moving forward. I recalled both travels and compared them. Each time it seemed as if I had returned to the present when I had spoken aloud. Could that be the key to being able to control the travel? Zelda would certainly possess crucial details to understand those journeys, but I would need to summon the courage to ask her.

Chapter Thirteen

Shadyside, Pittsburgh PA 2011

When Thomas and I entered Mom's room, Will was perched on the edge of a chair next to her bed. As soon as he noticed us, he sprang out of the seat, nearly knocking it over. Will's eyes were fixated on Thomas. He growled through clenched teeth, "I didn't know *you* were coming."

I was stunned at the gruff tone of Will's voice which seemed to be directed toward Thomas.

Thomas inhaled for several seconds, and I wondered if he might be counting to ten. Then he slowly released the trapped air. A reaction seemingly induced by Will's words. I couldn't decipher if it was his attempt to push away anger, regret, or sorrow. Thomas hesitated a few more seconds and then said, "I took a few days off to visit with Jade." He put his arm around me and nudged me in front of him, seemingly like a shield. "Aren't you going to welcome your sister?"

I stepped toward Will and extended my arms since he seemed to be frozen in place. We briefly hugged, and he muttered, "Good to see you."

"Likewise." My reply was as insincere as his greeting since he'd made no attempt to contact me since my arrival. I returned to my previous spot.

He patted Mom's hand, touched his finger to her nose, and warmly said, "I'll see you tomorrow." A gut punch to my memory of Sully which caused the scene to become even more uncomfortable for me.

Mom pleaded, "Can't you visit for a while?" She patted the bed indicating for Will to sit next to her. "Jade drove a long way to be here with us."

"Good of you to come. I'm glad you got here *safely*." As Will emphasized 'safely' he glared at Thomas. "But I really must get back to work. Important conference call in an hour." He nodded and scurried for the door.

I stared after Will as he exited the room and then looked to Thomas as I waited for some explanation. But it was apparent he did not want to talk about it—a reflection of my malfunctioning family. We never spoke genuinely or deeply about anything, never shared true feelings, and always tiptoed around anything meaningful or insightful. Obviously in full display by the secrets kept about Sully and Mom, Thomas' feelings toward Mom, Mom's feelings toward Thomas, and both of their feelings toward me. I never realized families were honest with each other or shared insights until I had caught a glimpse of it in Tiffany's family.

Occasionally, during passionate discussions, her parents' voices had raised to a fevered pitch toward each other, but at least they had expressed their feelings honestly. And as passionately as they had aired their views, they even more deeply conveyed reflections of love toward each other and especially toward Tiffany. She had always known that she was loved above all else. A feeling I ached for.

I attempted to pry information regarding Will's behavior from Thomas, but with no success. He changed the subject back to Mom and me. He asked her, "How was your therapy session today?"

"It was hard. I don't like it," She stuck out her lower lip and folded her left arm over her right casted one.

Her personality seemed to have changed quite a lot. Before the accident, she did not hesitate to speak her mind void of any filters. A trait some called bold while I found it hurtful and offensive. Since the accident, she appeared to be quite compliant with occasional childish mannerisms.

"Now Evie. You know the harder you work, the quicker I can take you home." Thomas rubbed her shoulders.

"You're taking me home today," she exclaimed.

"Soon. But not today."

She pouted.

He attempted to distract her, "How about a couple of sips of this yummy protein drink?"

111

She crossed her arms. "Yuk!"

He tried again. "I see you have pudding here left from your lunch. It's your favorite, chocolate."

"Mmmm," she smacked her lips.

"Do you remember Jade's friend, Tiffany?" He opened the pudding container and fed her a spoonful. "Jade, tell her about your lunch with Tiffany."

She nodded and opened her mouth indicating she was ready for another spoonful. Her nod was not really a reflection that she remembered my friend. Mom seemed to have forgotten big chunks of her past and Tiffany may have been included in the lost ones. I was surprised that Mom didn't react to the mention of Tiffany. Mom had adored her.

Even with occasional sporadic memories, there was no significant pattern as to which ones came to the foreground of her lobe and which ones may be forever lost. The doctors had said that time may be on her side.

Thomas had told me that she seemed to recall her and Thomas' high school crush but had no recollection of attending art school in New York. She had remembered that I had moved away but could not remember why.

Mom seemed more interested in the pudding than my story about lunch with Tiffany, so I did not follow his lead. Again, we did not stay long as our presence seemed to exhaust her.

On the ride home, Thomas explained that some days she seemed more confused than others. The doctors were not concerned since it was so soon after the accident and sometimes brain injuries took time to heal. They were hopeful that her memories and personality would return nearly one hundred percent. I secretly and selfishly hoped for less. Although I did not want her to remain childlike, I liked the gentler, kinder Mom. It was a relief not to have to tiptoe around her like she was an unexploded device.

However, I was mostly concerned with how thin she was. Thomas said that several years ago, Evie had lost her appetite and began shedding pounds. There had been no apparent physiological reason why she had lost her appetite. And the doctors at the time were not concerned with her weight loss that understandably followed.

When she had consumed the pudding earlier, it gave him some sense of hope that she would start eating again. She had hardly eaten anything since the accident, and the doctors suggested they might have to use alternative methods to ensure she gets the necessary nutrients.

I steered the conversation back to Will since I thought it would be easier for Thomas to talk in the car where we did not have to make eye contact. The pain of talking about it was apparent in his voice. He explained that he felt guilty about Mom's injuries, and it haunted him every day. In addition to his own self-blame, Will held him entirely responsible, doubling his guilt.

He explained that the evening of the accident he had driven her to an art exhibit but was too tired to attend with her. When it was over, he had suggested she take an Uber home so that he did not have to pick her up.

He had previously told me that the car she had been in got T-boned on Mom's side. I knew she had broken her arm and leg, but I had not been told that her head had smacked the side window, and she had sustained a severe concussion. I assumed he did not want to worry me and had hoped she would have recovered from the head injury before my visit.

"I'm sorry," I said. "You must know it's not your fault."

"My brain tells me it's not." He gripped the steering wheel tighter. "But my heart does not agree."

"Mom's very lucky to have you." I swiped at an escaping tear. "She didn't always appreciate all you did for us and I'm sorry, neither did I."

"Thank you for sharing that. Sometimes I look back and hate myself for the many mistakes I've made. A big one is not making any attempt to visit you these past three years."

"I own some responsibility for shutting you out."

"Maybe we both could have tried harder." He loosened his grip on the steering wheel. "If you don't mind talking about him, I'd like to know about Sully and the time you spent with him."

"I'd love to share that with you." I cleared my throat. "But first, I want to thank you for not abandoning Mom and me when I was born. I know most men might have, but you did not. I hope you have no regrets about that."

"Not one," he said emphatically.

Instead of going back to the apartment, we decided to stop at a coffee shop where we each got our favorite drinks, and then we walked to a nearby park. It was a lovely warm day with hints of autumn approaching. We found a bench with a few early leaf escapees resting on the boards. We brushed off the beautiful colors and sat facing each other. We talked honestly and openly, a first for the Fair family.

I explained the depth of hurt I felt knowing I had been deceived for most of my life. I also told him how angry I was that I was robbed of all those years with Sully.

Thomas justified his actions telling me he was madly in love with Mom since they were high-school sweethearts and would have done anything to get back together with her. He had never gotten over their breakup when she had moved to New York to pursue her art passion. So, when she had returned to Pittsburgh, he asked her to get back together. She agreed and for him, it was as if she had never left.

A few weeks later, she had discovered that she was pregnant and did not know how to get in touch with the father. Immediately, Thomas asked her to marry him anyway. She agreed but demanded they never speak of who the father was. He had justified the agreement by thinking it would be best to keep it a secret even though his gut told him it was not wise.

"Love can override sensible thoughts in your brain." He leaned closer to me, took my face in his hands, and said, "And for that, I am sorry for the deep wounds we've caused."

Thomas went on to tell me that after I was born, he believed and still did that the resemblance of me to Sully had caused Mom to resent her actions including marrying him. They had mostly gotten along and had made it work but were no longer naïve teenagers.

He cleared his throat, "So many times, I was tempted to tell you the truth, but my promise to her overrode the temptation." Thomas' voice cracked. He took a sip of coffee. "It was also a bit selfish of me to keep Sully out of our lives. I believed that Evie might still be in love with him, and I was afraid that she might leave me if she had ever located him."

"You've always been loyal to her, and I admire that in a human being." *Maybe Mom looked at me as a reminder of a love she couldn't have, but I still believed it was more than that.* "But it hurts that you didn't see my pain."

He looked at me with obvious sadness in his eyes.

"I spent my childhood trying to please her." I felt my pulse thudding in my wrist. "I thought it was my fault. If only I was smarter, prettier, funnier, then maybe she would like me."

Thomas averted his eyes away from me. "I now see how wrong I was. I can only hope that someday you will forgive me."

"I'm working on getting rid of the bitterness. It's held me back from pursuing a fulfilling life. As I work on that, I'm hoping forgiveness will follow."

"We are all flawed in some way. Some of us more than others. And our lives never follow a straight line." He looked down at his coffee and then directly into my eyes. "But I am truly amazed by you. You have proved to be quite a resilient woman despite what you've been through."

I reached over and squeezed his hand. No one, except Sully, had ever told me I was amazing.

He cleared his throat. "Don't think I'm trying to excuse her, but there's something I think will help you to understand Evie a little better. I was able to see through your mother's hardened exterior because I was witness to how her mother, your Grandma Gilda, treated your mother. When we had first dated, one of Evie's friends would have to pick her up so that we could go on a date. We'd meet at Isaly's for ice cream or the lake for a picnic. Once when we had met at a movie theater, one of your grandmother's friends saw us kissing. When Gilda found out, Evie was not permitted to even go out with girlfriends for months."

"I wasn't aware of any of that." I shook my head. "And while Grandma Gilda was not a particularly warm person, I had never witnessed her treating Mom so badly."

"She had mellowed a bit over the years and she and Evie sort of established a truce once your mom and I married."

"I'd been in grade school when Grandma Gilda had died so I understand why you would have kept that kind of nasty information from a ten-year-old." I was a bit shocked at the harshness of Grandma's actions toward my mother.

Thomas quieted his voice as if instead of remembering, he was back there, again. "The night of prom, Gilda took Evie's dress and locked it in a trunk. Your Grandpa Joe rescued it and drove Evie to the prom to meet me and her friends."

I stared at my coffee. *Regardless of that new information, she still had the power to end the train of abuse instead of continuing it with me.*

He picked up a leaf and twirled it in his hand averting his eyes from me. "If you do the math, Your Uncle Bern was born just six months after your grandparents were married. I believe Gilda did not want Evie to follow in her footsteps, so she was overprotective of your mom—overprotective to the point of abuse."

"I was going to be Evie's knight in shining armor, marry her, and whisk her away from the bad situation. Instead, she had decided to move to New York to attend art school. I left for college, and I think you know the rest."

My heart softened a bit for Mom, but I needed to be completely truthful about the woman he unconditionally loved. I explained, "When I arrived in Spring Creek and met Sully, it became clear as to the reason your wife's attitude toward me was not what a mother's should have been toward her daughter." I stared into Thomas' eyes to make sure I had his full attention. "I had thought she resented me for just being born, and now you think that maybe she still had feelings for Sully, and I reminded her of him. But I do believe that she was unjustly ashamed because of the lineage I'd gotten from Sully. The hue of Sully's skin was a shade darker than mine. My green eyes and my curls were a gift from him, too." My voice cracked, "Not only did she hide the fact that you were not my father, but she also passed me as white ignoring a significant portion of my heritage."

Thomas had nothing to say. Processing that new information, I supposed.

"I think what really hurt was that I knew I didn't resemble you or Will with only a slight resemblance to Mom. But each time I questioned it she always had a response. Even if it didn't make sense, I still wanted to trust her and you." I bit at my lower lip. "I guess I was waiting for you or her to tell me the truth." My voice lowered to a whisper, "the truth that deep down I had already suspected."

Chapter Fourteen

Shadyside, Pittsburgh PA 2011

Thomas appeared to be digesting the details regarding my mother's abhorrent deceitfulness. *Was he feeling what I had felt when I'd learned that I had been lied to for most of my life?*

I filled in some of the details that his wife had failed to reveal to her husband including how Sully and she had met in a pottery class while attending art school. Sully was in love with Evie, but right before graduation, she had ended their relationship with no explanation. Up until that point, she had not given him any reason to believe she had wanted the relationship to end. He recalled making plans for the two of them after graduation. But when he thought back, he realized she had never agreed to any of his potential arrangements.

I explained to Thomas that I believed that Evie hid behind a veil of hypocrisy to hide her prejudices. It appeared that it was okay to date him but living together was not an option, and marriage was definitely out of the realm of possibility. Sully and I both had thought that maybe she had been afraid of her parents not accepting him.

I realized from Thomas' reaction that his actions to be complicit in her lies may have stemmed from the fact that he was so in love with her that he did not press her for information regarding who my father was. Or possibly it was Evie's choice to withhold information from him and me because she wanted to erase Sully, New York, and art school from her life. Either way, Evie and Thomas had both wronged me.

I shared with him my first cherished Sully memory, "The moment I stepped into Sully's open arms, I knew I was home." I closed my eyes recalling his warm embrace. "We had twenty-seven years of catching up to do, and so we spent as much time together as possible."

Thomas remained silent, so I continued. "His preferred art medium was clay sculptures and pottery. He excelled at his craft but struggled to turn it into a successful career."

Other than an occasional blink, Thomas remained as still as a statue. I glanced at his chest to make sure he was still breathing.

Then I reminded myself to breathe. "After art school, to support himself, Sully got a job in a restaurant, learned every aspect, and worked his way up to chef."

Thomas' only movement was an occasional blink.

"When I met him, he was an established chef in a restaurant in a town near Spring Creek and was quite successful. We possessed a shared energy in the kitchen as he patiently taught me everything he knew." I smiled. "I felt accepted and loved. And that's why I never returned to Pittsburgh."

"I'm sorry I enabled your mother's lies." He swiped at a tear which had formed in the corner of his eye. "I had just wanted to keep the peace, so I'd never questioned anything. I was wrong. I'm so sorry, Jade. Please know that from the moment you were born, I loved you as my own, and I still do."

"Don't you see it's hard for me to trust my mother and I'm sorry, but you, too."

He nodded and then drooped his chin to his chest.

"Sully had been completely honest with me, even when the truth was difficult." I recalled his sincere eyes during our deep discussions. "He'd told me that he was proud of his lineage. We engaged in multilayered conversations about race and prejudices. He recounted all the major and minor things a Black man had to consider every time he left his house. Things I never thought about since I was a woman who had always passed for white."

Thomas shifted positions on the bench.

"I was never afraid to ask him anything. And for each intense dialogue, we had exponentially enjoyable moments, too. He was a kind soul, and through his example I saw the potential of how grand life could be."

Thomas listened; his eyes fixed on me.

"Besides cooking together, our favorite thing was to invent outlandish recipes for popcorn. We would try to outdo each other.

The only rule was that no matter how disgusting the popcorn looked, we each had to try it. Every Monday, on Sully's free evening, we would watch a movie and consume our concoctions.

He was passionate about life and could easily make me laugh. That's what I miss most, the laughter and especially the sound of his deep baritone chuckle."

"I'm so happy you have those memories to carry with you." Thomas cleared his throat, "I hope you can find it in your soul to forgive me. I am going to do everything I can to make sure you understand the love I hold for you in my heart."

I believed that he had always loved me and continued to. The desire to trust him hovered nearby, but it was going to take time for him to earn it.

"Sully's death nearly did me in. I felt I'd lost the only person I could trust."

Thomas looked at me with truthful eyes. "I'm sorry you had to go through that without family to support you." Then he lowered his head. "I did try to contact you a few times, but you never returned my texts or calls."

"I was angry, felt lost, and mistrusted everyone, especially you and Mom." I reached in my pocket for a tissue. "I was determined to rely only on myself."

"I should have driven across the state to see you. I should not have given up." Thomas rubbed his forehead as he shook his head. "I will regret that until the day I leave this earth."

"I'm sure Mom influenced your decision. And besides, you had to live with her."

"Yes. Absolutely. But ultimately, it was my decision not to act on what I knew was the right thing to do." He left out an overwhelmed sounding breath.

I surprised myself, but I reached over, hugged him, and said, "I'm so very sorry. I never considered that you were hurting, too."

Chapter Fifteen

Shadyside, Pittsburgh PA 2011

The next day, Thomas had planned to spend another day with me, but got an emergency call and had to go to work. I decided to laze around the apartment and remain in my pajamas. I contemplated visiting Mom but decided to wait until I could go with Thomas.

I was about to make myself lunch when I got a text from Will asking if I was free for lunch. He worded it so that I knew the invitation did not include Dad. I texted him that I was free and that Dad was at work. Will picked me up shortly after noon and we drove to a restaurant near Dad's apartment. The menu offered several vegan options which is why Will chose that particular eatery.

We were greeted as soon as we approached the host station. "Welcome back, Will!" The host extended a handshake toward Will. "And who is this lovely lady?"

"This is my sister, Jade." Will nodded my way.

"Well, welcome, Ms. Jade." The friendly greeter offered a handshake toward me. "Why hasn't Will brought you in before today?"

Will answered for me, "She's in town from across the state."

"I hope you are enjoying your visit." The host picked up two menus. "Right this way." He led us to a table next to the window where we had a view of the busy sidewalk as people hurried past, probably on their lunch break. "It is very nice to meet you, Jade. Please have Will bring you here again before you leave."

"It's nice to meet you, too." I did not want to tell him I would not be in town long enough to frequent his establishment again.

Will suggested a few vegan as well as nonvegan options. He said that he has tried all the vegan options and had never been disappointed. I assumed by the way the host greeted Will and by Will's knowledge of the menu that he was a regular.

Will confirmed my assumption. "I bring clients here a lot and occasionally I come for happy hour with the people from work.

I nodded. I felt even more distant than I had when there had only been miles between Pittsburgh and Spring Creek separating us. I knew very little about Will's work life and his social life. If we hadn't been half-siblings, I doubt we would have even been acquaintances.

Will ordered a vegan wrap with a side salad. I ordered the same wrap, but with a cup of barley soup. Before our food arrived, the waiter brought an appetizer of caramelized brussels sprouts. "Compliments of Henri."

"Please thank him for us." Will smiled.

I got the feeling that Will was not only well known but also well liked at that establishment. Thinking back to our school years, Will was the one always invited to parties and his personality afforded him the luxury of having an extensive friend group.

During lunch we kept conversations very light and avoided subjects that might cause tension between us. I was grateful that he had invited me and did not want to ruin what might be an attempt to bridge the gap between us.

When I finished the last delightful bite, Will said, "I'm going to have a coffee. Would you like some tea? They have a nice breakfast blend."

I was quite pleased that he remembered my favorite tea. "Only if you don't need to hurry back to work."

He glanced at his watch. "I've got plenty of time. This has been nice."

He smiled and I returned his smile. And then my smile abruptly faded. From where I was seated, I could see the host station. Nicholas walked in, stopped at the desk, and embraced a tall, gorgeous blonde.

I hadn't realized I'd gasped until Will said, "Are you feeling okay, Jade? Your breathing, it's shaky."

127

I stared at my empty plate hoping Nicholas hadn't seen me. "I'm fine. I'm fine."

"Are you sure?"

"Mm, hmm" I could feel the perspiration beads forming at my hairline. I continued to stare at the table until two pairs of shoes stopped next to us. I let my chin tilt my head toward the figures. It was Nicholas and the blonde.

"I thought that was you, Jade. It's good to see you." Nicholas nodded. "Will, good to see you, too."

I was too stunned to say anything, but Will said, "Nicholas. It's been a long time."

"You remember Patricia, from high school." Nicholas waved his hand in front of her as if he were a game show host. "She's in town for a conference. Small world. Isn't it?"

I almost choked on the air I'd inhaled. It was Patricia and boy did I remember my frenemy who made my high school years unbearable. I stared at her features and squinted in an attempt to connect her with the image I remembered from years ago. Then my imaginary spotlight focused on her hair which is why I had trouble recognizing her at first. In high school, her hair had been a dull brown with a dirty-blonde hue, not the creamy buttery blonde she sported in front of us.

"Won't you two join us? We were just about to have coffee and tea," Will offered. I suppressed the urge to kick him under the table.

Patricia spoke first, "Thank you so much for the offer, but I'm meeting some friends from the conference." She turned to me and said, "It was great seeing you, Jade." She turned and waved toward a table of six other men and women. "Bye, Nicky! Loved seeing you."

Nicholas waved as she left and then turned to us. "I really wish I could stay, but I'm just picking up lunch for the office, and they will hunt me down if I'm late with their food."

I nodded relieved that he could not stay. "We wouldn't want that to happen. Looks like your order is waiting at the front desk."

He turned to Will, offered a handshake, and then placed his other hand over that one. "Really great to see you. I hope you're doing well." Then he turned to me and extended his hand.

I reached up to offer a cordial handshake. He held my hand, placed his other hand on my elbow, and before I realized what happened, I was standing facing him. He embraced me and whispered, "I'm so delighted to see you."

He gently kissed one of my cheeks and I assumed he was going for the other, so I turned my head. Awkwardly though, we turned simultaneously, and our lips met. He kissed me. The scent of his cologne took me off guard and I momentarily felt a pleasant emotion bubble up from the past and I returned his kiss. Then I stepped back from his embrace and moved to the other side of my chair using it as a safe barrier.

Will cleared his throat with a sound people make when they are in an awkward situation. What he didn't know was that it was awkward for me, too.

Eyes focused only on me, Nicholas asked, "Can we possibly get together while you're in town? Maybe we can have dinner some evening?"

I hastily replied, "No. I'm leaving in a few days, and I need to spend time with my family." I hoped that my emphatic "No" and my abrupt response ensured that he understood the kiss had been a huge mistake.

When it looked as if he was going in for another hug, I extended my arm at full length, shook his hand, and said, "You'd better go before they send the search team for you." He nodded and headed for the front desk.

The waiter approached the table. I sat still stunned at what had just transpired. Will order our drinks and requested the bill.

Will chuckled, "Well, that was awkward."

I had to laugh, too, because if not, I was afraid I might cry. "I know. I shook my head. I immediately regretted returning his kiss."

"I could tell by your body language. However, I'm not so sure he interpreted it the same way."

"Well, I'm leaving in a few days and luckily I will not have to run into him again."

After Will dropped me off at the apartment, I decided to connect with Carl since it had been a few days since I'd last spoken with her. I was curious of how Winnie was doing and how Jim's recovery was going. Also, I wanted an update on Carl and Phoenix's relationship. At that time of the day, Carl would be at the law firm, so I texted her asking her to give me a call when she got a break. I'd barely hit send when my phone buzzed.

"That was fast," I answered. "Aren't you at work?"

"I took the day off to support Winnie until her daughters arrive," she said.

"Wait. What's going on?" My stomach tightened.

"Jim had another stroke early this morning." Carl's voice cracked. "They don't think he's going to make it."

"How's Winnie holding up?" I closed my eyes and said a quick prayer.

"She seems eerily calm," Carl said. "Not like the last time when she was a wreck." Carl continued, "She asked me not to call you. She didn't want you to leave Thomas and your mother."

"That's so Winnie." That time, my voice cracked.

When Thomas returned after work, I explained the situation in Spring Creek.

He responded, "You ought to be with your friend." He continued, "Your mother will be in the rehab facility for several more weeks, so there's not much you can do here to help in her recovery."

"But I—" I began.

He interrupted, "I have friends here to lean on and especially Fred. We've been friends since we were sixteen years old. He's seen me through some of the toughest times."

I don't think he meant to make me feel guilty for the years I was silent from them. No matter his intention, I felt a slight pang of guilt.

I remembered the scene of Marguerite's sixteenth birthday where she and Lilloise seemed to be such close friends. I was sure they would have had a relationship like Thomas and Fred where they could depend on each other. Even though I wasn't sure if they were real, my heart ached for them, and I wondered if they had ever gotten to see each other again.

Thomas' voice brought me back to the decision I had to make.

He continued to try to convince me. "And hopefully I'll be able to work things out with Will."

"I'll see if I can talk some sense into him," I said with minimal belief that it could be possible.

"This Winnie sounds like a special person and it's important to be there for friends who need you especially in times of crisis."

He said that he would be okay if I left. But I made him promise that he would call if he needed me to come back.

"Like I promised, I'm going to be completely honest with you from now on, even if it's difficult and means going against your mother's wishes." He hugged me and held on like he did not want to let go.

I returned the hug. "I'm not sure if the damaged bridges between us can be repaired, but I'm willing to try."

"Thanks for being honest with me, Jade," he squeezed a little tighter.

Neither of us backed away. He took advantage of the pause to give me a little fatherly advice. "Cherish those friends of yours. They sound like good people." He kissed the top of my head. "Now go create the life only you can imagine. And don't forget, I'm here for you if you need me. I love you, Jade. I have always loved you."

"I love you too, Dad," I whispered.

Chapter Sixteen

Spring Creek 2011

"How do we hold on to hope when sadness permeates our lives?" The minister closed his eyes briefly. "Here's what we do, we follow Jim's example of his intense love for life. And we thank God to have known Jim even if only for a short while."

Whispered amens scattered throughout the sanctuary. In the crowded pews, heads nodded in unison.

"He was a quiet man, but never hesitated to talk about his love, Winnie."

I could see Winnie a few rows up and across the aisle, her daughter's arm wrapped tightly around her. Winnie dabbed at her tear-streaked cheeks. I felt like a sponge absorbing Winnie's loss. Her visible sadness combined with my memories of the pain of losing Sully was too much to bear. Even the best memories of Jim and Sully were of no comfort. The feeling of loss overtook everything, and memories just intensified my grief. I wanted to run and hide, escape the boulders that threatened to crush me. But I remained frozen in the pew. Either out of respect for Winnie, or fear of diverting attention to myself, I wasn't sure which. Maybe it was commitment to a friend that outweighed my need to escape. I stifled a sob as I thought about Jim and Sully and how their zest for life was cut short and we were robbed of time with them.

I wondered why Winnie's faith didn't seem to be shaken during Jim's illness and ultimately his death. I know mine would have been. One time when I had dropped off food at her house, she had looked close to being defeated. I had asked her how she kept going and she had said, "My faith gives me hope. For without hope, I have nothing. Hope makes it possible for me to continue even when I'm ready to give up. I'm not saying it will be easy, just possible."

Carl reached over and squeezed my hand. Somehow, she sensed that I needed to be reminded of how important friends were and that we weren't going through this sadness alone.

The minister spoke as if he were inside my head, "His passing reminds us to hold closely to those you love, to not take life for granted, and to take those leaps of faith."

I may have imagined it, but it seemed his eyes were fixed on me like he was speaking directly to me. Each word resonated like Thomas' guiding words and Sully's advice regarding friendships. *Take those leaps of faith.* His words lodged in my skull and reverberated over and over. Then the minister read a Bible verse which was drowned out by the persistent words in my head, and I barely heard the soloist as she sang *In the Garden.* After the refrain, my thoughts wandered to Lilloise. I had so many

135

unanswered questions. Since my last snow globe travel, curiosity had surfaced poking and prodding me to satisfy it. I decided it was time to take that *leap of faith*.

When I arrived at the Weary Travelers' Antique Treasures, the door was locked and the sign in the window turned to Closed. I cupped my hands around my eyes and peered inside, smashing my nose into the glass. Disappointed as I couldn't be sure I'd have the confidence to try again the next day, I turned to go.

Steps away from the door, I heard Zelda's familiar sing-songy voice. "My darling Jade Fair," she called.

I stopped on the sidewalk, and she hurriedly caught up to me. She extended her arm to offer her hand. "It's been a while. So good to see you. Please come in." She unlocked the door.

"I'm sorry to disturb you. Don't reopen just for me." My voice wavered as my confidence faded.

"Don't be silly. It's indeed a pleasure to welcome you back." She held the door open for me to enter first. "You've been away too long."

My eyes followed her red spikey hair up and down with each nod. And in typical Zelda fashion, her outfit looked as if a color party had exploded on her floor-length dress.

She smiled and said, "How might I assist you, darling?"

"I was thinking…I thought…Well, I'd like to look at and possibly maybe purchase a…" I stammered.

"I know exactly the perfect snow globe for you." Zelda scurried away. As if she had read my thoughts, she returned with the small ornately decorated globe from Paris. Zelda confidently handed the globe over to me unlike previous visits when she seemed to mistrust me.

I ran my fingers over the elaborate carvings around the base highlighted by gold etchings. It was exactly as I had remembered it. The miniature Louvre sat among the frothy cloud of snow.

I thanked her, paid with the cash from my emergency envelope, and left her shop clutching my purchase as if it were a dear friend. In my apartment, I found the perfect spot on the end table right between Sully's pottery piece and his urn. They were visible from anywhere in the room.

I spoke to my new purchase, "I'm not sure if I need Zelda or not. But, when I get enough nerve, I will visit you, Lilloise and Marguerite." I sighed. "I promise."

And then the minister's words reverberated, *Take that leap of faith.*

****

Paris, France 1927
In front of the Louvre Museum

As if no time had passed, I was right back at the scene of Lilloise's sixteenth birthday. Her father had her by the elbow leading her away. She was crying and pleading with her father to let her stay in Paris.

"Please Papa, Marguerite's family has invited me to live with them and finish my studies here." She twisted her body, attempting to break free from his grasp. "I promise I will return to the States as soon as my school year is over."

"Marguerite's people don't have the same values as us." He grabbed her by both arms, pulled her close, and growled inches from her face, "I forbid you to have any further contact with them."

Lilloise's pleading turned to a whisper, "Please Papa, please." She sounded defeated.

"I should have never let your mother talk me into bringing you to Paris." They walked farther away from Marguerite. "I knew I would regret it."

Lilloise twisted her neck to enable her to see Marguerite until they turned down another street and out of sight.

Marguerite sat on a bench next to a woman I assumed was her mother. She stroked Marguerite's hair, attempting to console her. Their conversation was in French, but even though I could not understand what they were saying, the pain on Marguerite's face was apparent. Her mother's visible empathy was evident through her tone and body language. *Clearly, a mother who truly loves translates the same in any language.*

"I wonder what that must feel like," I whispered. My words, although spoken softly, wafted toward the bench. They made eye contact with me, and then I was clutching the globe on my own couch.

Chapter Seventeen

Lake Wallenpaupack 2011

Serene was the exact word to describe the scene painted by the countryside in the middle of the state. The landscape's beauty spoke, 'All is right with the world.' That's what I imagined it said as I gazed out the car window. Trees on either side bending toward each other seeming to create a tunnel as we drove through. *Nature's tunnel...amazing.*

"You okay back there?" Winnie glanced in her rear-view mirror.

"Yep," I nodded. "Just enjoying the view." However, in my heart, I knew that everything was clearly not right with the world. Jim was gone, Winnie was still grieving, and I felt helpless not knowing how to support her. She had lost her best friend. Once, she had told me that while she and Jim deeply loved each other, their partnership was cemented more in friendship than by love. Winnie and Jim had been tethered to each other by a visible link which stemmed from that deep friendship. And now their bond had been permanently severed by his death.

The other difficulty weighing on me was that Mom was still in rehab. While she had not gotten any worse, her recovery was far slower than the doctors had predicted. Not helping the situation was that Will continued boycotting any genuine conversations with Thomas thereby leaving Thomas to rely on friends instead of family.

Also, gnawing at my thoughts was Lilloise and Marguerite's sad story coupled with the fact that I did not know for sure if they had ever seen each other again. Even with all that occupying my mind, I attempted to model Carl's positive attitude. I welcomed the view and embraced the opportunity to spend time with these two ladies in order to get to know them better. A valiant effort put forth by me in an attempt to welcome a new attitude.

"We've about another hour or so." Winnie turned down the music a few notches. "I really appreciate you girls giving up your weekend to help me."

Carl sang along with the chorus of a song on the radio adding her own version. "We need love, lots of love. And we love Winnie. Yes, we do. Yes, we do. Yes, we do." She belted the words off key and made the song her own.

We chuckled and joined Carl in singing a chorus of, "Yes, we do."

We need lots of love. I tossed that thought in between my ears…love of a partner, love of family, and love of friends. My mind wandered to a conversation I'd had with Sully. He had said,

"You can't live in a vacuum, Jade. No one can, at least not for long."

He had been encouraging me to at least be open to new friendships. But what frightened me the most was that he thought I needed a friendship group like he had. That would have required me to be open to being vulnerable. So, I had replied, "I'm not alone. I have you."

To which he had stated emphatically, "You need friends, too. Girlfriends who you can relate to."

I had named Winnie and Carl, but he had harrumphed and had said, "A few ladies who you know not much more than their names. Do you know anything about their lives, or have you shared any part of your life with them?"

He was not wrong, but at that moment in my life, I had all that I'd needed. It was before he had gotten sick, but maybe he'd had a sixth sense about his future and my being without him.

Sully had gone on to remind me about his friends that he would meet at the park every Wednesday morning. They would play chess and then have lunch together. They had been friends ever since he had moved to Spring Creek. And when he had found out about me, he could not wait to share the news with them. They had even bought him pink balloons to congratulate him like he was a new dad, even though I was in my twenties. But technically, he was a new dad.

Sully and his best friend, Roberto, had supported each other on the yearly anniversaries of each of their wives' deaths. And Roberto would take a pilgrimage with Sully to Sully's wife's gravesite in upstate New York each year on the anniversary of her birthday.

Winnie shook me from my thoughts, "You girls are awfully quiet. Especially you, Carl."

"Enjoy it for it most definitely won't last." Carl laughed. She was admittedly honest.   Winnie and Jim owned a cabin on Lake Wallenpaupack a few hours from Spring Creek. Jim had mostly used it as a fishing retreat. Winnie was not so much an outdoorsy person. She had said that was what kept their marriage together for nearly thirty-five years. They had done most things together, but each had their own interests, too. While Jim had fished, Winnie had been content to cozy up to a rocker on the front porch with a novel in hand.

Since Winnie did not plan on using the cabin without Jim, she decided to put it on the market. She wanted to get it ready to sell and also prepare it for winter. She asked if we would go with her to help. We had gotten a late start after work, so it was almost dusk when we arrived. It was a bit rustic, but cute for a cabin. We grabbed our weekenders and the bags of food and got settled in.

The sun had nearly set causing the daytime temperature to drop quite a bit. Winnie fixed a fire in the huge fireplace since she said the furnace would take a while to kick in. There was a large pile of wood that Winnie said Jim had chopped the last time he was there.

"I'm going to chop some more wood," Winnie said. "It doesn't look like there will be enough to get us through the evening."

There was plenty, but I figured Winnie needed some air. The visible pain on her face was probably caused by her memory of the last time she was here with Jim. We could see her through the window. She handled the ax striking the log like she had the strength of three humans. Getting out her frustrations I supposed. I hoped it helped ease her pain.

She returned carrying a load of firewood and dropped it near the fireplace with a crash. Obviously, her anger, or sorrow, or frustrations, or all three, were still at the forefront. I wondered if the grief of losing a spouse was as difficult as losing a parent.

I asked, "Where do you want us to start?" I hoped cleaning would help distract her.

She inhaled, exhaled, and flopped into an overstuffed chair. "Let's just enjoy the evening," Winnie said. "We can get to cleaning tomorrow."

"Sounds like a plan," I agreed. All that chopping must have helped release some anxiety. "I know it's early, but do you want to get into our jammies, make some popcorn, and sit in front of this cozy fire?"

"And maybe a little hot toddy to warm our bones?" Carl held up a bottle of rum accompanied by a big cheesy grin.

"You always bring the essentials, Carl." Winnie laughed.

It was so good to hear her laugh. That may have been the first time she had laughed since before Jim had gotten sick. She had been through so much, so I was determined to make the weekend a respite for her. Carl and I had decided earlier that we would help Winnie get everything done in one day. Then she would be able to relax the remainder of the extended weekend.

Our office was to be closed on Monday to honor Mr. Gladman's grandfather who had founded the law firm. Every year Mr. Gladman closed the firm on the anniversary to commemorate his grandfather's accomplishments. That meant we had a three-day weekend to not only help Winnie, but also enjoy some quality girlfriend time.

The fire crackled, we donned our comfy pajamas, and had an overflowing bowl of popcorn which could have fed an entire football team. I gazed at Winnie and Carl. They seemed content. Even Carl was quiet. I liked that feeling of supporting a friend and hanging out with girlfriends. *Girlfriends. They are my girlfriends.*

I smiled, which quickly turned to trepidation at the thought of wanting to be part of the group but realizing that belonging required being vulnerable. I silenced that thought momentarily because I was trying hard not to go down that dark hole. Besides, it was nice just sitting together in a cabin in the quiet of the woods, and I did not want to ruin it with negative thoughts.

As we sat in the silence, maybe in thought, maybe contemplating our lives, maybe being grateful, maybe thinking of the future, a peacefulness enveloped me. I was sure the crackling fire, the tranquil surroundings, and the lack of everyday noises, contributed to the calm feeling.

Carl broke the silence, of course. "What's your favorite memory of your childhood?"

She's going to make me go there.

"That's easy," Winnie chimed in first. "Every year a few weeks before school started, my mom would take me on the bus to town. She'd let me pay the fair as she'd said, 'Like a big girl'."

She smiled. "We'd go downtown and shop in the largest department store, the one that had twelve floors. Each level would have different items from furniture to clothing to jewelry. And one floor had shoes. Can you imagine, a whole floor for shoes? We'd ride in the shiny brass elevator with an elevator operator who wore white gloves. We'd stop at the floor with children's clothing. She'd let me pick out my first day of school outfit, and then we'd go to the shoe floor, and I'd pick out a new pair of shoes."

Winnie looked away as if she was right back in that store. She smiled. "We'd eat at the Ticky Tock Clock, a restaurant on the top floor of the department store. We'd request a window table with an expansive view of the city. It had white tablecloths, white

146

cloth napkins, and fresh flowers adorning the center of each table. I'd order a Shirley Temple and Mom would get tea." She sighed. "It was a magical moment with her. She always made me feel so special."

Carl pointed at me. "Your turn."

I shoved a handful of popcorn into my mouth. Chewing very slowly, I shrugged and pointed to my mouth indicating I was unable to talk.

"Okay. I'll go." Carl threw one kernel in the air and caught it in her mouth. "Mine has got to be when I was about ten years old, and my mom let me do her hair and makeup. I was going through the 'I'm going to be a makeup artist' phase."

Great. Both mom stories.

"It looked like I had readied her for a starring role in a zombie apocalypse movie." Carl chuckled. "And she actually praised my horrific artistry and then encouraged me to pursue a career in it. She was probably aware that that dream would eventually fizzle like all my other ones."

I grabbed another handful of popcorn and stared at the fire hoping they had forgotten that I hadn't taken a turn.

"You must have so many stories running through your mind that it's difficult to come up with just one," Carl teased. "Or maybe you just don't like to share."

Carl was correct. I did not like to share. Exposing my past to others was frightening because once it was out there, I could never take it back. There was no backspace key in conversations. And once others know of my traumas, they will forever label me as pathetic, lonely, friendless, sad, etc.

I finished chewing, swallowed, inhaled leisurely, and said, "Well, this one time my mom gave me a trunk that had belonged to my great grandmother. She'd used it when she had sailed to the U.S. from Wales. I'd always admired it, and when my mom redecorated her bedroom, she set it out on trash day. When I asked if I could have it, she agreed to let me put it in my bedroom." It was kind of a stretch to be considered a favorite childhood memory, but it was all I could think of. It made them smile, possibly out of pity.

"Speaking of redecorating, could either of you use bedroom furniture?" Winnie asked. "I was thinking of turning one of the spare rooms into a study. Also, if you know of anyone who works on cars, I'd like to donate Jim's tools to a newbie just starting out. Jim would have wanted that. But not his woodworking ones. I enjoy working with wood."

"What have you made with wood?" Carl asked.

"I built that bookshelf in my living room."

Carl whipped her head around from staring at the fire to staring at Winnie. "You build furniture? Why did we not know that?"

"I haven't had the time to work on anything lately. But I was thinking about maybe building a coffee table with a glass lid to display some of Jim's Army medals and memorabilia."

"I didn't know you were so handy. You're amazing," Carl exclaimed. "What other secrets are you hiding?"

"No secrets. You know me. I'm an open book." Winnie looked my way.

I tried to blink away the tears that were betraying me.

Winnie must have noticed because she said, "Are you okay, Jade?" She leaned in toward me. "You're so quiet. You seem to be hiding from something."

I shook my head.

"Sometimes if you keep things bottled up, eventually you'll explode."

My secrets were bubbling inside of me like a volcano ready to erupt. I blurted out, "This is a picture of my dad and me." I held up my phone with the photo of my dad and me on my screen saver.

Winnie's expression told me that my outburst may have been a shock to her. "Okay then," she said.

Carl frowned. "Okay then," she repeated Winnie's words.

The guilt I had been carrying exploded like an overfilled balloon. The truth was that I felt like a fraud. I hated my mother for passing me as white, and here I was following in her muddy footprints.

149

Winnie reached for my phone to probably lessen the awkwardness. "Let's see the man who gave us the lovely Jade."

Carl glanced over Winnie's shoulder. "Oh. He's cute. I see where you get those gorgeous green eyes."

Winnie exclaimed, "That's Chef Sullivan!" She looked from me to the phone and back to me. "He's your dad?"

I nodded.

"He was the chef at my and Jim's favorite restaurant." Winnie handed the phone back to me. "We always celebrated special occasions there. His creations were not only delicious, but they were also works of art."

Tears filled my eyes. I blinked, scolding them to be gone because I knew that if I let one escape, there would be no stopping the rest.

"What a small world," Winnie continued. "We'd wondered what had happened to him. The only thing the restaurant would tell us was that he no longer worked there. Something about confidentiality."

Winnie knew about Sully's memorial service, but I guess I hadn't mentioned his name. I told Winnie about Sully, his health struggle, and the whole story about my mom and my stepdad. Since Carl had already heard most of that story, I tried to condense it as much as possible. Then to be sure they both understood the depth of hurt that my mother had caused, I confided that for twenty-seven years, she had hidden the fact that I was mixed race. She had passed me as white only.

I told them that when I had learned the truth that she had hidden Sully, my biological father from me, I had been devastated. She had not only lied, but in doing so, erased a great portion of my heritage. My relationship with my mother had always been a sort of tango of mostly me unintentionally irritating her and then me responding with a constant need to convince her to like me. Her disdain for me still echoed in my soul. It had been impossible not to feel small around her.

Unlike Thomas who had been stunned into muteness, Winnie and Carl came to my side and embraced me.

"You must have been so angry with her and Thomas," Carl said.

Winnie hugged me tighter. "I'm so sorry you were robbed of time with Sully."

They understood. And that's all I'd been longing for.

Chapter Eighteen

Lake Wallenpaupack 2011

We were three ladies in a rowboat as still as Lake Wallenpaupack united in silence. I was entranced by the serenity of the moment as my thoughts wandered to Lilloise's and Marguerite's seemingly infinite bond.

I supposed Winnie was thinking about embarking on a new chapter without Jim. I was sure she did not wish to turn the page, but it was not in her power to turn back time. My heart ached for her.

Carl, a contented smile adorning her already pretty face with her back to the bow of the boat, sat perched on the seat like a queen on her throne. I silently crowned her "Queen Wallenpaupack." *Was she as positive and upbeat on the inside as she presented herself to the world?*

Not surprisingly though, my thoughts were interrupted by Carl. She paused an otherwise tranquil moment with another one of her thought-provoking questions, "Any regrets?"

Winnie sighed. "Of course." She hesitated for several seconds and then said, "I thought Jim and I would have more time together." She squinted into the distance as if searching for her beloved. "We included as part of our wedding vows that we would make an effort to appreciate each other every day."

"That's a tall order." I harrumphed.

She scrunched her nose at me. "Jim and I enjoyed the challenge. We didn't always succeed, but the attempt was never far from us." She sighed. "However, I do regret not trying harder during the busy years with the girls when life pulled us in all different directions."

She continued, "My biggest regret though, was not spending more time with Jim here at the cabin. I never saw this place like he saw it, like I do now. When I did join him, I failed to fully enjoy myself because my commitments at home consumed my thoughts." She scanned the shore as if she was surveying the perimeter of the lake. "I wish I would have made more of an effort to look through his eyes instead of through mine. I thought of this place as a small rustic cabin in the woods away from civilization." Tears welled up in her eyes, "It's too late that I appreciate it now."

We sat absorbed in the stillness. As I digested her regrets, I compared them to my current and past relationships.

She sniffled. "I have an even bigger regret, though that no one except Jim knew."

My eyes swelled open like two frog eyes as I anticipated a big confession from her.

She maintained an even voice, "When I went away to college, I broke it off with Jim because I wanted nothing to tie me down. I wanted to party and date without guilt. And party, I did."

Carl and I glanced at each other. I shrugged as I found it impossible to picture sensible Winnie partying.

Winnie placed her hand on her chin as if in deep reflection. "It's only a partial regret though because the positive outcome was that those failed relationships led me back to Jim. Those other guys made clear what I did not want in a partner. Until then, I hadn't realized that Jim was like the Northern Star, and I needed those unsuccessful experiences to recognize that I needed to follow it back to him. Luckily, he waited for me and never pushed for details. He was a saint."

Winnie's story reminded me of Thomas unconditionally accepting my mother back into his life with all her baggage.

"Carl, you asked the question, you should go next." I attempted to avoid self-reflection.

"I would have to say that I don't have many regrets because I've learned so much from my mistakes, more than I'd have learned without them." She smacked the water with the paddle sending ripples gliding outward from the boat. Carl became eerily quiet.

After several uncomfortable moments she spoke, "Now I regret asking that question." Her voice cracked, "I had a baby when I was sixteen." Carl stared at the bottom of the boat as if she were drilling a hole with her eyes, maybe wanting to sink it so she would not have to finish.

I glanced at Winnie to see her reaction. Her expression was stoic.

Carl continued, "When I told my parents, they'd said I was to tell no one, not even the father, until they could 'figure out what to do with me.'"

I winced at those biting words.

"They had sent me to live with my grandparents on their farm in another county." She swiped at a tear. "They threatened that if I told anyone they would disown me. It seems they had been more concerned about their church people finding out rather than my wellbeing and the baby's."

Winnie shook her head. "I'm so sorry, Carly."

"I had the baby too early. She only lived for a few hours. I got to caress her in the infant ICU. I named her Lovely. And my grandma held Lovely and kissed her tiny forehead. All my grandpap could do was cry. He said he felt so helpless. When I called my parents, they'd said that it was my fault because I was an evil girl, and it was God's way of punishing me."

Carl's body shook as if two tectonic plates had shifted beneath the boat. It was shocking to see optimistic Carl so visibly upset. She must have wanted to confess or else why would she have asked such a personal question of us? I was at a loss for words. This is where we would count on Winnie for motherly advice, but she sat silently still.

Finally, Winnie stood up and took a step toward Carl. The boat rocked. I grabbed the sides for I was sure it would tip. The rocking mimicked the feeling I felt. Winnie sat on the bench next to Carl, embraced her as if to anchor her, and said, "You don't believe them, do you?"

Carl shook her head. "It still hurts though, that they had been more worried about their friends instead of me." Tears streamed down her face and glistened with the sun's reflection. "I finished my high school years living with my grandparents on their farm and have never set foot in my parents' house. And I never intend to, ever again." She hurriedly sucked in air as if it was briefly passing by and she was afraid she would miss it.

Pride filled my soul to be in the company of these two strong, confident, hopeful women who were willing to expose their vulnerable human sides. I felt a connection to them and no longer felt alone.

Back in the cabin, we were cozy around the fireplace for our last evening at Winnie's camp. The scent of hot chocolate filled the room, and I was wrapped tightly in a red wool plaid blanket like a swaddled infant. I welcomed the contentment which swelled over me until Carl lobbed a pillow at my head.

She must have realized I had not yet shared a regret, and her determination to not give me a pass manifested in her scolding words, "Jaaaade. You have a way of avoiding getting real with us."

I played coy. "Whatever do you mean?"

Winnie joined Carl in the friendly attack and freed the couch of all pillows by sending them my way. I counter attacked by aiming the soft ammunition at the two of them, but to no avail. I was outnumbered.

Accepting defeat, I searched for a story that would not cause me remorse after the telling. I pondered confessing my time travel, but I no longer regretted that. I also realized they probably wouldn't believe me and think it was a ploy to avoid sharing. I opted for a story about regretting not taking more time off work to spend with Sully during his final days.

"I'm sorry I wish I'd have known what you were going through during Sully's illness." Winnie clutched her hand to her heart. "I would have been there for you."

"I know you would have, but I was so secretive."

"At the time, I wondered why you had always left work so hurriedly. But you were so private I didn't want to pry." Winnie's eyes projected empathy.

"I mistook your silence for being unsociable." Carl shook her head. "Just goes to prove that you never know what someone is going through."

Feeling lighter with that minor confession, I continued, "I also have pangs of regret for blaming Thomas for my mother's transgressions." I sighed. "When I was in Pittsburgh, he had told me that he understood and did not blame me. But I have guilt feelings for how harsh I had been toward him and how I'd shut him out of my life. We had some honest conversations, and I had realized how selfless he was and still is. It was the first time I had felt connected to someone in my family other than Sully."

Carl scrunched her face and asked, "I'm wondering, didn't you ever question why you didn't resemble either Thomas or Will?"

"I had asked my mother several times, but she'd always divert the conversation and make me feel I was being silly. Or she'd refer to a distant relative of Thomas whom I had never met and say that they had similar looks as me." I shook my head remembering those discussions and how uncomfortable she had made me feel just for asking. "Once when I had asked if I had been adopted, she showed me my birth certificate which clearly had Evie's and Thomas' names on it. And then she'd said, 'End of discussion.'" And so it was.

"I'm proud of you, Jade," Winnie remarked. "You've really opened up to us this weekend. It warms my heart that you trust us with your innermost feelings."

I nodded as words of thanks were stuck in my throat. I was still a work in progress. It wasn't easy, but that weekend with

Winnie and Carl inspired me to continue working on my trust issues and to build strong lasting friendships.

The following shortened work week flew by. Not because it was shortened, but because my job seemed to be more tolerable having closer friendships there. We had always known that Winnie had our backs, but now we were a strong group of three supporting each other. We were far more connected than the three of us had been before our cabin weekend. I started to understand why Sully had been so persistent that I find reliable friends. His wisdom continued to support me, and for that I was amazed and grateful.

Chapter Nineteen

Spring Creek 2011

Awake and dressed before noon on any Saturday was not in my typical repertoire. However, when I had awoken at seven a.m. and could not go back to sleep because I found it impossible to turn off my brain thinking about the past weekend with Winnie and Carl, I decided to get on with the day. While showering, I recounted the trip to Winnie's cabin and mentally detailed the strength that each of those women possessed. I felt a bond with them and compared its similarities to Lilloise and Marguerite's bond. All four of those inspiring women gave me hope.

As I pushed my scrambled eggs around my plate, I thought about friendship and hope. I drew strength from all four of their stories and their lives. I scooted off the counter stool, grabbed my coat, and headed for the door. As I walked the few blocks, I felt empowered with each step. Quite a contrast to formerly avoiding that street, I power walked to Zelda's store. I needed answers to questions, and only Zelda could provide them.

In my hurry to get answers, I had not thought about how early it was and that her store would not open for another hour. Instead of returning home, I walked to the park to organize my thoughts. I found peace in the brisk morning air and contentment as the sun warmed my face. The cooler nights seemed to have changed the leaves a bit from just a few days before. The emerging colors were beautiful, and I could almost hear them say, 'The best is yet to come.'

I watched as two children collected acorns and then made their way back to whom I guessed were their parents sitting on a bench on the other side of the patch of yellow and gold mums. The girl followed a little boy who seemed much younger than her and she scooped up the acorns that had fallen from his tiny hands. They dropped the gathered acorns into a bucket and ran back to the base of the white oak to collect more.

I wondered what they planned to do with their collection. Once at a craft fair, a crafter had glued acorns together to create seasonal wreaths and picture frames. I imagined the fun that family was going to have crafting with the acorns. How lucky those children were to have parents making such enjoyable memories with them.

Walking in the park had been one of my and Sully's favorite things to do. Sometimes we had walked in silence and absorbed nature's sights and sounds. Other times, we had shared a favorite bench and told stories from before we had met. Once he had encouraged me to contact my mother and Thomas. When I explained how deep the wounds went, he said that he understood and never brought it up again.

I felt peaceful remembering him sitting beside me. Tilting my head toward the sky I marveled at the clear aqua sky next to the palette of autumn's early colors. I spoke to Sully in a whispered voice even though no one was near enough to hear me. I told him how grateful I was to have had him in my life, but that I missed him every day. I especially needed his advice and encouragement more than ever.

With Sully's spirit filling my soul, I felt more centered as I walked to Zelda's. When I entered her store, she seemed deep in conversation with a customer. Zelda's average height was dwarfed by the man. His unbuttoned overcoat exposed broad shoulders and a slim build.

I perused the nearest display of antique lamps and admired the one with the hanging crystals. *This might be my next purchase.* The thought caused a chuckle to escape as I remembered the first time I had entered Zelda's store and had thought the antiques were nothing I would ever want to acquire. However, with a change in perception, I was able to view the antiques in a new light.

The lamp with the most hanging crystals caught my eye, and I imagined the numerous rainbows the clear gems might create with the morning sun peeking through my apartment window. I was sure there would be a magnificent display of colors across the otherwise dull room. It could certainly be a great way to boost my mood each morning.

I continued to browse, waiting my turn. Her customer's voice was soft, but his words floated to my curious ears. "Since I've arrived in town, she's done nothing but ask for that particular one. I've taken all the globes I still have in my possession, but she just shakes her head and pushes them away." He set a box on a nearby table. I could see that it contained several of the snow globes. "I appreciate you letting me take these to her, but just like the others, she pushed these away and again shook her head."

Zelda gazed into the box like it contained a litter of kittens. She stroked them and smiled.

"I'm now regretting encouraging my father to sell part of her collection. She had so many snow globes, especially the ones from Paris, that I didn't realize the effect the missing ones were going to have on her. If I'd have known how upset it was going to make her, I never would have told him to pare down the set."

"Don't you worry. We'll certainly find that special one that just might be a comfort to Lilloise."

I was sure Zelda had never mentioned that the woman who owned the collection was named Lilloise. I was quite certain I would have remembered that. *It couldn't possibly be a coincidence.*

"Most days she's not fully lucid, but when she is, she's adamant that I bring her that particular one." He took out his wallet. What appeared to be a business card fell to the floor. When he bent over to pick it up several locks of his brown curls went

163

rogue over his left eye. He tucked it neatly back in place behind his ear and then handed Zelda his card. "She keeps mumbling something about a Marguerite."

A noise slipped from my lips. It was not one I had ever heard before. At first, I did not realize it had come from me until they both glanced my way and then Zelda winked. Perspiration beaded on my forehead, and my breathing set an abnormal pace from trotting to full blown galloping.

I spun around to hide my angst and in so doing, I knocked into a display of hats hanging from a coat rack. Several of the occupants tumbled to the floor. They scattered and I scrambled to pick them up. I could feel my face burning from my neck to my forehead. I was certain I had turned ombré shades of red as the embarrassment climbed its way to my hairline.

Zelda's customer rushed to assist my fumbling attempt at gathering the scattered hats. He smiled and handed me the two he had collected. His smile exuded empathy rather than mockery. "Here you go," he said as he brushed off the purple felt hat. "No harm done." His voice was like a warm breeze calming my embarrassment.

The long lashes which curved above his mesmerizing deep blue eyes caused me to lose my breath, and I was unable to even sputter a thank you. I walked backwards to return the hats to their perches and knocked into the rack again. This time I caught it, and thankfully no more collateral damage occurred.

His broad smile created a deep dimple on his left cheek. It might have appeared to unbalance his face, but this stranger was handsome enough to sport just one. Two might have caused my knees to weaken.

He returned to Zelda, and I was finally able to breathe. He asked her, "Would you please contact me if you locate it? I'm hoping it will bring some peace to my grandmother."

"Certainly," Zelda replied. "Before you go, I'd like to introduce you to Miss Jade Fair." She emphasized the word 'Miss.'

I turned to see her wave me toward them. I hesitated since I was sure my face was still flushed. Her wave became almost violent. She called, "Jade, I'd like you to meet Mr. Milton…" She glanced at the card in her hand, "Mr. Walter Milton, the Third. Hmmm, the third." She lifted one eyebrow.

I was still embarrassed, but I knew Zelda would persist, so I stepped toward them and extended my hand to the gentleman. "Nice." The words in my brain hesitated to travel from there to my mouth. "to you…I, I mean, nice to meet you." I felt like a silly schoolgirl that had just been asked to the sixth-grade dance. I pointed to the hats. "Thank you."

He nodded and smiled with his captivating blues eyes. "It's my pleasure to meet you."

I composed myself enough to get a complete sentence out. "I'm sorry to have eavesdropped on your conversation." I took a breath and cleared my throat, "But is your grandmother the former owner of that lovely snow globe collection?"

"Yes. She'd collected them over the years." His smile broadened. "She was obsessed with the Paris globes and had traveled there sometimes several times a year. She'd purchased a different one each time."

"I may have the one you're looking for." I demonstrated the size with my hands. "It's of the Louvre."

"That may just be it," his voice rose. "Would you be willing to sell it to me?"

"I'd be glad to let you borrow it to see if it's the one," I said. "If you need to keep it, then we can work something out."

"I can meet you here tomorrow, take it straight away to my grandmother at The Willows Nursing Facility. It's not too far from here. I'll either bring it back if it's not the one or give it to her and purchase a replacement for you."

I quickly calculated a plan to be able to meet her. "It might be easier if I meet you at The Willows."

"That's very kind of you. You remind me a lot of my grandmother. She is thoughtful like that. But I don't want you to go out of your way."

I explained that my father had been a resident at The Willows for quite a few months where I had gotten to know several of the nurses. I had been meaning to visit them, and therefore I could fulfill a promise I had made to keep in touch. Although that was true, my ulterior motive was to meet Lilloise.

We exchanged cell numbers and agreed to connect at The Willows the next day at ten o'clock. Out of the corner of my eye, I saw Zelda fanning her hands wildly and stopping just short of clapping. She had a huge grin plastered across her face.

Chapter Twenty

Spring Creek 2011

The anticipation of the next day's meeting caused me to have a nearly sleepless night. I pieced together all the new information I'd received yesterday. *It has got to be the same Lilloise.*

I did not know if I would be able to recognize her as she had been quite young in my travels and according to Zelda, was one hundred or nearly that.

The image staring back at me in the full-length mirror said that jeans, a blouse, and a blazer appeared too casual. So, I switched the jeans for a pair of black slacks. Still not good enough to meet Lilloise. I tried again. On the third attempt, I donned a floral skirt, topped with a pink sweater and knee-high brown suede boots.

"Perfect," I said. The reflection agreed with a nod.

I met Walter Milton in the lobby of The Willows Nursing Facility. He was impeccably dressed, but not in a show-off way. He wore tan pants, a navy sweater, and a white collared shirt beneath the sweater. His brown curls were neatly tucked behind his ears.

He smiled when I walked through the entrance doors and approached with an arm extended. "Jade Fair," he said. "Thank you again for your kindness."

He held my hand and placed his other over it. My hand felt like a pearl inside a clam shell. He said, "I hope this trip was not too inconvenient."

Let's see. My big plans were laundry and grocery shopping.

"No. Not at all." I smiled and enjoyed the warmth of his hands and prayed my face would not betray me as it had the day before. "As I'd said yesterday, I've been wanting to visit the staff here and this is a perfect opportunity."

"I'm hoping this will satisfy my grandmother and minimize her frustration."

I patted the canvas bag hanging from my shoulder. "Would it be okay if I went with you to give her the globe?" I held my breath hoping for a 'yes.' "I'm anxious to meet her."

"She loves visitors. Just keep in mind that her dementia prevents her from holding a reasonable conversation." He paused. "And most times she doesn't remember who I am and thinks I'm some nice man who visits her. So, she'll probably think you are a lovely lady who is visiting her, too."

I was flattered that he had called me lovely and tried to suppress the flustered feeling. After a few moments of uncomfortable silence, I composed myself and said, "Thank you, Mr. Milton for allowing me to meet her."

"Please. Call me Walt," he chuckled. "Only my students call me Mr. Milton."

I was just about to ask him where and what he taught when a voice behind me said, "Girl! It's about time you visited us."

I knew the voice. It was Dad's favorite nurse, Effie. She hugged me from behind before I could turn. "How've you been?" She spun me around. "It's been months."

"I can't complain," I said. "Still living in Spring Creek and trying to get by." I pulled a box from my bag.

"You remembered my favorite, Sarafini's chocolate covered pretzels." She pulled my face to hers and planted a kiss on each cheek.

I turned to Walt, "This is Effie. She was my dad's favorite nurse."

Effie smiled, "And Sully was my favorite guy. I miss that man. Never complained. And he had every right to."

I nodded and frantically blinked to avoid a gush of tears. Any mention of him still had the power to produce a downpour.

She directed the conversation toward Walt but gave me a quick squeeze. "This gal was one dedicated daughter. She never missed a day visiting her dad."

An unruly tear escaped and slid down to my cheek. I hoped that if I didn't whisk it away, no one would notice, and so I let it travel to my chin and hang onto it as if it were about to fall from a cliff.

Walt slipped a handkerchief into my palm.

How sweet. I've never known a man who carried a cloth hanky.

Effie did not seem to notice the tear or the hanky. She said, "Be sure to treat this one well. She's a gem."

Walt cleared his throat. "My grandmother is expecting us, so we'd better be on our way. It was very nice to meet you, Effie."

This stranger is turning out to be a real gentleman. It seemed he didn't want to correct Effie. Her assumption that we were a couple might have embarrassed her so instead, he quickly excused us from the situation.

"Nice to meet you, too," she reciprocated. "Who did you say you are here to see?" she asked.

Walt replied, "My grandmother, Lilloise Milton."

She must be in the other wing. I've not met her. But on my break, I'll be sure to stop and say hello."

As we walked away, Effie called after us scolding me again for not visiting often enough. Then Walt and I proceeded down the long hallway to Room 110. With each step, my heart thumped in my ears. It was impossible to contain my excitement and nervousness with the thoughts of meeting Lilloise. I hoped Walt could not hear the tha-thump, tha-thump pounding in my ears.

Walt entered Lilloise's room, and I stood in the doorway. She sat in a wheelchair, her shoulders slightly hunched; her hands folded in her lap. White wisps of delicate hair framed her face. Her skin appeared almost translucent, and her eyes were fixated on her hands. I searched her face for some recognition of the Lilloise from my travels.

"Grandmama. There's someone I want you to meet." He took my hand and led me to her chair. "This is Jade. Jade Fair."

She sat up a bit straighter. Her eyes squinted as she studied my face. "It's you!" she exclaimed. "Where's my Marguerite?"

As if there was a lack of air, I lost the ability to breathe, and then my voice abandoned me, too. *Did she recognize me as if I really visited Paris and was not just hypnotized?* My head swirled and I grabbed the edge of a table.

Walt shrugged "Grandmama. We don't know a Marguerite."

Lilloise pointed at me and said, "She does. Find me Marguerite. Find my Marguerite"

Walt attempted to change the subject, "Jade has something I think is going to please you."

She turned her head and stared out the window where a squirrel frolicked on a tree branch readying for winter. Walt nodded toward my bag. I took out the snow globe and handed it to him.

"Gram. Look what Jade has brought for you." He placed it on the table next to her bed.

Tears streamed down her porcelain skin. "Marguerite. My Marguerite," she clutched her curved fingers and brought them to her chest.

Walt positioned her wheelchair closer to the table. Her thin, wrinkled fingers clasped around the snow globe as if she was holding the moon. She raised the globe and caressed it with her cheek. "I've missed you terribly."

Walt probably assumed she had missed the snow globe, but I was certain she longed for Marguerite.

Walt closed his eyes and whispered, "Thank you."

A chill circulated throughout my body as sweat simultaneously formed at the brink of every pore. My heart rate quickened and so I excused myself to avoid an anxiety attack. "I have a few other nurses to visit. I'll let you have some time alone with your grandmother." I turned for the door.

"Jade, wait," he said. "Meet me in the lobby shortly? We can discuss replacing your snow globe."

I nodded. On the walk back to the lobby, I steadied myself, hugging the tiled hallway wall while attempting to process what had just happened. Trying to compose myself, I repeated a mantra. *Just breathe, Jade. Just breathe.* My life had been turned upside down ever since Zelda had emerged in it. And this was proof that something unexplainable had been happening.

173

As I approached the nurses' station, I spotted Effie, Liz, and Phillip huddled around a computer screen. I credited them for the excellent care my dad had received during his stay at The Willows. Effie spotted me first. "There she is," she jumped up. I braced myself for another massive hug, but Phillip got to me first.

They filled me in on their lives. Phillip had just returned from his honeymoon in Hawaii. Liz was pregnant with her third child and looked as if she would deliver at any moment. Effie said that she was working on a PhD in nursing administration and had two more years to finish. They shared many more details, but those were all I gleaned since my focus remained back in Room 110.

Liz's and Phillip's breaks were over, and they had to resume their duties on another floor. They hugged me together in a sandwich squeeze and told me to please visit more often. It was time for Effie to do her rounds. She embraced me, tapped her finger on my nose, and said, "Now promise me you won't be a stranger."

"I promise," I said.

Effie hesitated before letting go. She whispered, "I'm sure you know your dad was the best."

I nodded.

"You are so much like him." She stepped back. "I'd better go before we start bawling our eyes out."

As I said goodbye to Effie, I noticed Walt in the hallway gazing at us. After Effie had gone, he smiled and then approached. "I was just admiring how well liked you are."

"Those nurses are exceptional people, the way they've dedicated themselves to care for these residents. I thanked them every day when my dad was here. They were just grateful that someone noticed."

"Thank you again for giving your snow globe to my grandmother. I'm sorry she seemed to upset you. But after you'd left, the globe gave her some peace and she genuinely seemed comforted." He pulled his keys from his pocket. "If you're not in a hurry, I'd really like it if you would join me for lunch, and then we can go to the antique store, and you can pick out a replacement snow globe."

I was unsure if I could be capable of being good company since my scrambled mind tried to sort through what had happened with Lilloise. But my desire to know more about her outweighed my angst. So, I agreed to have lunch with her handsome grandson.

Chapter Twenty-One

Spring Creek 2011

My rusted second-hand car, which I had named Mortifié (French for mortified) or Morty for short, begrudgingly followed Walt's blue Volvo. Of course, Walt's car matched his beautiful eye color. Whereas my rust-colored car blended with the actual rust on my car's dented passenger door. At the first stop sign, my embarrassed Morty sputtered nervously—an apology for sharing the same road as the immaculate Volvo.

At Tressa's Tuscan Cucina, I parked in the slot next to Walt's auto. Side-by-side, Morty seemed even more pathetic. Walt waited for me at my car's bumper, and then we walked toward the restaurant. Due to Walt's apparent kindness, I was spared humiliation as he never smirked nor raised an eyebrow at my ratty vehicle.

After we were seated, Walt started the conversation, "Again, I'm so sorry my grandmother's reaction to you was upsetting." He cleared his throat. "But as I told you at the nursing home, I witnessed her demeanor completely change. The snow globe seemed to be a calming influence far better than any sedative." He smiled. "It's difficult to explain, but I've not seen her that content in a long time."

I could have explained. But not knowing him very well, I was hesitant to do so.

Walt shifted the conversation to a more neutral subject which allowed me to push aside my conflicting feelings of whether to confess or not. He said that he lived in New York City, was a professor at NYU, and he taught courses in nineteenth century French Literature. He was only in Spring Creek for the weekend to visit Lilloise. Whenever possible, he tried to visit every few weeks.

He explained smidgens of Lilloise's married life. There had been rumors in the family that it had been an arranged marriage because both his grandmother and grandfather had come from wealthy families. Neither Lilloise nor Walt's grandfather had ever shared many details, and Walt's parents had discouraged him from inquiring.

Walt's opinion was that his grandparents had had a strained marriage and had mostly lived apart. She lived at their estate several miles outside of Spring Creek most of the year while her husband lived in their brownstone in New York City.

"As a young boy, I was happy to not have to share my grandmama with anyone and never questioned why she mostly lived apart from my grandfather."

177

I buttered a knotted dinner roll and tried to picture Walt as a young boy.

He went on to tell me that he had spent many summers with her at the estate. She was kind and he had learned lifelong lessons from her. She told him that he was lucky to live in a time when his parents could not demand he live his life as they desired. Her advice to him was to never waver from his convictions.

"Grandmama had taken many trips to France. On one occasion when I was about ten years old, I accompanied her. We visited a town just outside of Paris." He hesitated. "She had said that she was looking for an old friend."

I asked, "Did she find the friend, and did she ever mention the friend's name?"

"No. I don't recall," he replied. "I was young and was more interested in ice cream cones, and I remember a parade celebrating... hmm, I think it was honoring the harvesting of grapes." Walt chuckled.

I chuckled, too. I imagined a parade of everything cloaked in purple.

"I have a most vivid memory of my first taste of wine." He smacked his lips. "Grandmama told me not to tell anyone. And I never did, until now." He winked.

"Do you think she might have been searching for Marguerite?"

"That's possible." He stroked his clean-shaven chin as if a beard resided there. "If there really is a Marguerite and it's not a person created by her dementia."

I wasn't sure if Marguerite was an apparition or not. But because of what had happened in Lilloise's room, I was closer to believing I really did have an encounter with the two ladies. I could not possibly tell Walt what had really happened. He'd think me ridiculous since logic and reason said it was impossible.

The waiter placed Walt's shrimp scampi in front of him and the pasta primavera in front of me. It not only looked delicious, but the aroma which wafted upward teased my senses and invoked an olfactory dance in my nostrils. It ignited loving memories of Sully. I closed my eyes and imagined I was sitting across from him—a time travel I would most certainly cherish.

Walt cleared his throat, and I quickly opened my eyes to the reality that it was Walt and not Sully across from me. However brief, the momentary vision warmed me, and I smiled.

"It's so nice to see someone appreciate cuisine as much as I do." He smiled back at me.

It seemed unnecessary to explain that it was a memory and not the food which had triggered my smile. So, I just nodded.

He continued with stories about his summers spent with his grandmother. I was interested to learn more, but my thoughts kept returning to Lilloise asking me to find Marguerite. I hadn't realized

I was inattentive and staring off until Walt said, "Jade. You seem to be somewhere else. Is something bothering you?"

"It's nothing," I replied.

"I've found that when someone says the word 'nothing,' it is always something. And most times it's a big something."

"I apologize." I appreciated his empathetic expression. "It's been a long day and I'm trying to process what your grandmother said to me."

"Don't forget that Lilloise is mostly not fully lucid." His shrimp-filled fork dripping with butter stopped just short of his lips. "So, try not to be bothered by her asking you to find whoever Marguerite is. She seems to mostly live in the past and sometimes makes no sense at all."

I nodded, not in agreement, but to let him know I was listening.

"I'm truly sorry that she upset you," he said.

"No. I'm fine. Really." I smiled. "Now tell me more about your summers with your grandmother."

Even though the rest of the lunch was pleasant, I was mentally exhausted from the morning's event and asked if we could meet another day at Zelda's to purchase my replacement globe. He was leaving the next day, so instead he said that he would leave a credit card number with Zelda so that I could purchase another globe at my convenience. I thanked him for lunch and for sharing stories of his grandmother.

When I arrived home, I was relieved that my cozy apartment was a respite from the world. I needed time to process the day's happenings and be alone with my thoughts. Exhaustion set in, and my think-time soon became nap time. I awoke a few hours later curled up on the couch and still buttoned into my coat.

On my way to the office on Monday, I passed by Zelda's. There was a sign on the door stating that she was closed until Wednesday. I assumed she was on a trip to another auction.

Midafternoon, Winnie asked Carl and me to have dinner at her house that evening. Winnie appeared extra pensive, and I wondered if in addition to mourning Jim, something else was upsetting her. The rest of the workday dragged on as worry about Winnie consumed my thoughts.

Before going to her house, I stopped by Greene's Market and picked up some flowers to cheer her up and thumbprint cookies for dessert. I also purchased ingredients to use later that week to replicate the pasta primavera I'd had at Tressa's Tuscan Cucina. Although Carl and I had prepared meals for Winnie when Jim had been ill, I had been neglecting to cook for myself. It seemed too much trouble to plan dinner for just one, besides it reminded me that I could no longer share the kitchen with Sully. But I was determined to invoke the Carl method and replace sadness with beloved memories. So, I told myself it was time to get back into the kitchen, experiment with recipes, and create new dishes that would have made Sully proud.

When I arrived at Winnie's, there was a realtor's sign which appeared to have taken up residence on her property. *Are you kidding me!*

I sprinted up her front porch steps. The front door was unlocked, so I let myself in and called, "Winnie. It's me."

"In the kitchen," she replied. "Come on back."

Winnie was reaching for plates on a shelf when I entered the kitchen. Before she could say hello or turn around to face me, I squawked, "You're selling your house?" Even though I already knew the answer to the rhetorical question, I asked it anyway. The sign had made it quite obvious.

She placed the plates on the counter and walked toward me. "I'm sorry about that," she grimaced. "I'd asked my realtor to wait until tomorrow to install the sign, but I guess there was a miscommunication. I wanted to tell you myself."

"Where and when are you moving?" I asked. "Please tell me you've found a smaller place here in Spring Creek."

"Let's wait until Carl arrives." She dug through a lower cabinet and produced a cut glass vase. "And then I'll tell you both."

As if on cue, we heard, "Hey guys. Where are you?"

"Come on back, Carl," Winnie called. "We're in the kitchen." She placed a tray of asparagus in the oven.

I filled the vase with water and arranged the white mini carnations and snapdragons bouquet.

"I didn't know what you were having, so I brought a bottle of each." Carl placed two bottles of wine on the counter. "What's with the somber faces?"

"You didn't see the sign, I assume." I arranged the cookies onto one of Winnie's matching serving dishes.

"What sign?" Carl held her hands facing toward the ceiling as if we were going to toss the answer like a volleyball.

Winnie interrupted, "Let's get dinner on the table, and then we'll talk." She handed me the plates and silverware. "Set the table for me, please."

Carl shrugged. "What can I do to help?"

"The wine goblets and water glasses are in the China cabinet in the dining room."

"Okey-dokey. I can do that."

When I entered the dining room, I paused and looked around realizing there was no longer any trace that the room had formerly been converted into a bedroom. Every piece of furniture including the cabinet, side table, and grandfather clock appeared to be back in their original places. Carl scooted past me and removed the goblets from the cabinet holding them up to the light. She seemed to be admiring the hue cast by the light shining through the blue glass. *She finds joy wherever she can.*

When dinner was ready and we were seated around the dining room table, Winnie explained that with Jim gone the house was too much for her to take care of. She had thought about downsizing and renting an apartment. But then her daughter had asked if she would consider moving closer to her and to Winnie's grandchildren. The thought of being near her grandchildren was an opportunity too great to resist. She was going to wait to resign from the law firm until her house was sold. I secretly hoped it would be months or maybe even a year before that happened.

Carl and I listened as good friends do, but inside I ached. *Yet another person deserts me.*

Chapter Twenty-Two

Spring Creek 2011

Anxious to obtain the replacement snow globe Walt had promised and possibly get some answers from Zelda, I stopped by her shop after work on Wednesday. The closed sign remained on the door. I realized my mistake. I had read that she was to reopen on Wednesday, but I had failed to read the entire notice. She was closed until the following Wednesday. I would have to wait another week.

Impatient for answers, I decided I'd visit Lilloise. However, when I pulled into the parking lot of The Willows Nursing Facility, I spotted Walt's car. That was not a good sign since he only visited on weekends due to his teaching schedule. I said a quick prayer that all was okay. Not wanting to interfere, I decided to ditch my plan to try to obtain information from Lilloise.

Instead, I texted Winnie and Carl to see if they could join me for dinner. Carl had plans with Phoenix, but Winnie said she was available. We decided on the restaurant, Silk Road near her house.

When I arrived, Winnie was already seated and waved me over. She had ordered some shrimp rolls, shrimp dumplings, and a pot of tea and had already poured us each a cup. A perfect treat on such a chilly evening.

"I'm so glad you called," she said. "I was busy cleaning out a closet and hadn't planned ahead for dinner."

"Sorry it took me so long to get here." I slid into the booth. "There was an accident on the interstate, so traffic was backed up."

"The interstate?" She furrowed her forehead.

"I was over at The Willows Nursing Facility." I hoped she wouldn't ask for more details and would accept my explanation.

"Where your dad used to live?" she asked.

"Yes." I opened the menu and tried to divert the potential questions, "What looks good?"

It didn't work. She asked, "Were you visiting someone?"

"It's a long story." I acquiesced, "Let's order and then I'll explain."

After the server took our order, I gave Winnie the Cliff Notes version, careful to leave out the time travel episodes.

Winnie was mostly interested in the Walt portion of the story. "You had a lunch date on Sunday at a romantic Italian restaurant and failed to mention it to us the past three days?"

"It was not a date," I protested. "He was just thanking me for giving his grandmother the snow globe."

Winnie had an impish smile plastered on her motherly face.

"Someone like Walt could never be interested in me." I reached for a shrimp roll. "He's a professor at a university and I'm a college dropout."

"You don't need a degree to be successful," She began her allocution. "If you want a degree, then go back to school. If you want a different career, then create a resume. If you want a relationship, then don't write it off before it even begins."

I knew there was a lot of truth to her words, but most times, things just didn't go my way.

As if she knew my thoughts, she continued, "You can't just wait for your life to magically happen. You can be empowered by your own choices." She took my hands in hers. "Picture your life filled with excitement and joy, and where at the end of the day your heart is content. And then ask yourself what you need to do to get there."

I sighed. I had not thought of it as me waiting for life to happen even though I had never felt in control. I devoured a shrimp dumpling and savored her words. Cautiously I opened the door just a crack and allowed her wise comments to trickle in. I had no rebuttal, so I asked myself, *What would I need to do to get there?* And then I answered, *Trust that not everyone will deceive or desert me.*

Winnie took a dumpling and then passed the appetizers back to me. "If you can't yet picture it, keep searching until you're able to see it." She held the dumpling up as if toasting me with it. "Then don't walk toward it, run as fast as you can."

Friday morning, happy that I had almost made it through another week, I stirred my coffee, added extra sugar for a boost, and contemplated my next move. I wanted to text Walt to see if Lilloise was okay, but I did not want him to know I saw his car in the parking lot. I was afraid he would think I was too bold going to visit her without him.

As if Walt knew I was thinking of him and his grandmother, my phone buzzed. It was a text from him informing me that Lilloise was not doing well, and he was in town. He would be at The Willows by her bedside all day, but his father was flying in from California and Walt would need to pick him up later that evening. He asked if I could meet for coffee before he had to head to the airport. Always considering others, he asked what would be convenient for me.

Since the Coffee Coffee Coffee House was walking distance from my apartment and still on his way to the airport, I suggested we meet there. He said he could meet me there at eight that evening.

As I got ready for work, I anticipated a long day ahead with the coffee meeting consuming my thoughts even though it was twelve hours away. My emotions bobbed up and down like a buoy in rough waters. They went from excited that he wanted to meet with me, to sad regarding Lilloise's disintegrating health, then they soared to pleased that I would unexpectedly be sharing time with him, and finally to disappointed when I realized the reason that he had asked me was that I was probably the only one he knew in Spring Creek.

Before leaving for work, I stopped at my full-length mirror and repeated Winnie's words, "If you want a relationship, don't write it off before it even begins." I winked at the woman with newfound confidence. At least she was trying.

At the law office Carl asked what my weekend plans were, and I told her about the upcoming coffee meeting. Winnie caught the end of our conversation.

"Friday night date?" Winnie teased.

I began to protest, but Winnie held up her hand palm toward me interrupting my negative thoughts.

On my way home after work, I noticed the note on Zelda's door was no longer there. Hoping for some answers, I entered and was greeted with the enthusiastic Zelda cheer, "Jade. Jade Fair. It's so lovely to see you, darling" She clapped like an excited child and her smile widened.

I believed her words and enthusiasm were exclusively for me and not something every other customer was treated to. "I thought you were to be closed until next Wednesday." I approached the counter.

"Sometimes plans change, my dear." She winked. "I had a feeling it was more important that I return here."

She is a peculiar woman. That's probably why I've grown to like her.

"I'm looking to replace the snow globe that I gave to Mr. Milton." I scanned the shop for the globes. Panic bubbled in my stomach as I did not see them anywhere.

"I'm having some furniture delivered and I didn't want them to be bumped and potentially broken, so I moved them to a back room." She danced from behind the counter, her skirt flared as she spun. "Is there a particular one that interests you?"

"I was thinking maybe that one from France of a palace-looking building. It has two symmetrical stairs curving up to the front door with a façade that stretches the entire width of the snow globe."

"Mais oui, the Château de Fontainebleau," Zelda responded. "That's one of my favorites." Zelda hugged herself, closed her eyes, and smiled.

She has said that about each one of them. I returned her smile.

I scanned the store while she went to retrieve the globe. The antiques which I had originally little to no interest in, I now admired. I realized there may be intriguing stories connected to each piece. And it was fun inventing stories linked to the furniture and tchotchkes.

Seated in the wine-colored velvet wingback chair, I imagined a distinguished elderly gentleman with a vintage hand-carved pipe pursed between his lips. The sweet aroma emanating from the pipe would combine hints of vanilla and crème caramel. He would be contemplating the mysteries of life.

Next to me was the wooden and scrolled metal coat rack with several ladies' hats dangling from its hooks. I envisioned Sully's mother returning from church and delicately placing her hat on its assigned hook. Hers would be the small cylindrical one. Its' simple but elegant style was constructed of purple felt, had no brim, and had a flat level top. I knew her only from Sully's stories and a few phone conversations, but I felt the purple one matched her personality. I chuckled remembering knocking the hat rack over scattering its contents to the floor on the day when I had first met Walt.

There was a roll-top desk with the finish worn from the edges of the wooden top. I assumed it was worn from previous owners lovingly stroking its inlaid wood. Not knowing much about wood types, I chose it to be made of an exotic wood like rosewood instead of a common oak. It seemed it had been well used and loved as a practical piece of furniture in its prime. It housed several compartments including drawers and shelves. I imagined there were secret notes that might have been hidden in the tiny nooks

191

and slots. I wondered what other correspondence had graced the desk over the years.

With the invention of text messaging, writing desks had become obsolete. I lamented at the thought. I was certain that the previous owner would surely be disappointed to think that grandchildren and great-grandchildren would not be privy to ancestors' thoughts and experiences through handwritten letters.

Zelda returned from the back, ending my imagination game. "This is a beauty." She admired it before setting it on the counter. "I'll wrap it up for you."

I was about to ask her what she knew about Lilloise and the snow globes. I hadn't quite thought of how I could ask her about the time travel without sounding ridiculous. So, I just took a chance without knowing exactly what to say. Her back was to me which made it a little easier not being able to see her reaction. "Zelda." I whispered, "Have you ever felt like you were somewhere other than where you are right now?"

Zelda hummed a haphazard tune and tapped her foot a bit off beat. She either had not heard me or was evaluating my question. I immediately had regrets. Sweat beaded on my forehead while my nails dug red crescent moons into my palms. A bell tingled and I wondered if the ringing was a warning that I was about to faint. It rang again followed by the closing of the front door. A customer had entered.

Zelda placed my purchase on the counter, winked, and hesitated before handing it to me. I scooped my treasure into my arms, thanked her and headed for home.

While preparing salmon and a salad dressed in olive oil and red wine vinegar, Winnie's words echoed in my head, "You can't just wait for your life to magically happen."

I ate my dinner and gazed at my newly acquired snow globe which I had placed in the empty spot where the one that I had given to Lilloise had been. At the sink, while I washed my dinner dishes and skillet, Winnie's voice was strong in my thoughts, 'Picture a life where you are excited, joyful, content.' I dried the last of the utensils as her words grew louder. 'Ask yourself what you need to do to get there.'

I confirmed my fears aloud, "I'm frightened." I sucked in as much air as my lungs could hold. "But I need to know what happened to Lilloise and Marguerite." The volume of Winnie's voice grew deafening, 'Don't walk toward it, run!' I tossed the dish towel onto the counter and hurried to the globe. I stared into the orb housing the Château and gently rocked it back and forth.

****

Fontainebleau, France 1981

Across the street from where I stood was a lovely building with maroon and white striped canopies atop two large windows. The wording printed on the canopy covering the intricately carved wooden door said, Hotel de Londres, Fontainebleau. A woman emerged and I recognized her to be Lilloise. She had aged quite a bit, but her features were still recognizable. I guessed her to be in her early seventies. A young boy about age ten hung onto her handbag suspended from the bend at her elbow. He gazed up at her as if she were the most precious gift he had ever received.

I remembered a sermon I had heard in my youth. The minister had said that even though we know it is there, you can't see love like you can see an object. He had gone on to say that you can't touch love like holding a gift in your hands. He was wrong. I could see the love between Lilloise and the boy. There was a force linking them as if invisible ribbons traveled between them, bonding them, connecting their souls.

Petite Lilloise with many silvery streaks gracing her hair, smiled down at the boy who I was sure was young Walt. She patted his hand. *You can touch love.* His long wavy hair peeked out from under his cap and flowed to just above his shoulders.

They crossed the street, and I followed them, careful to not get too close. They proceeded down Rue Dénecourt past the Municipal Theater of Fontainebleau. Lilloise and Walt paused where Rue Dénecourt intersected Rue Grande. A small carousel with a giraffe and several other animals spun round as children squealed. Walt pointed and clapped.

They continued down Rue Grande and stopped at a tiny garden with a fountain. Lilloise paused to let the boy feel the cascading water. Next to it was a restaurant, Le Franklin Roosevelt. I chuckled. Then immediately covered my mouth afraid they might have heard me. I warned myself to not make another sound mistake as I did not want to abruptly leave them.

They paused at a church. Lilloise briefly bowed her head, and then moved on. After two more blocks, we passed a quaint little café. Several bicycles leaned against the weathered brick façade. Red café chairs matched the red striped canvas awning. Above the awning sat an ornate black wrought iron catwalk. On the patio, people relaxed as the sun warmed their conversations.

I followed for several more blocks until they stopped at a two-story cream-colored stucco building with a green patina door and matching green patina shutters flanking each of the six windows. Lilloise clapped the door with an ornate looking door knocker. From where I stood, the brass knocker appeared to be a lion with its mouth wide open.

A smartly dressed woman answered. From my vantage point I could only hear snippets of the conversation. From Lilloise I heard her say, "Marguerite." The woman shook her head and Lilloise repeated, "Marguerite. Marguerite Béatrice Matisse." With each word she increased the volume and added "adresse." The French word, adresse sounded a lot like the English word address.

The woman repeated Marguerite's name and again shook her head. She shrugged and called after them, "Je suis désolé."

From the look on Lilloise's face, I assumed désolé meant 'sorry' and she could not help with an address for Marguerite.

The boy took her hand into his tiny hand, kissed her hand, and said, "It will be okay, Grandmama."

In between Lilloise's muffled sobs, I heard her say, "Oh Walter. I'm afraid I've lost her forever."

He buried his head into her side. She hugged him closer.

My heart ached so badly. I longed to be back in the comfort of my tiny apartment. "Home, home, home," I called. Lilloise snapped her head my way.

My request was granted. I was in the safety of my home.

Chapter Twenty-Three

Spring Creek 2011

As I walked the few blocks to the Coffee Coffee Coffee House, a crisp wind caught the hood of my coat forcing it off my head. A chill traveled down my spine. Nearing the coffee shop, I marveled at how many thoughts had passed through my brain during the short walk. *I may never know if Lilloise ever reunited with Marguerite* was the last one that played over and over as if my brain had hit a rewind button. It might have been the falling temperature or quite possibly the thought of Lilloise permanently separated from Marguerite that caused the tingling to take the trek back up my spine and then down once again like a speeding elevator.

When I entered the coffee house, Walt was seated at a window table with two steaming mugs of tea. He must have remembered our last conversation when I had said that tea warms my bones on chilly evenings.

He stood as I approached the table. "Thank you, Jade, for joining me." His words drifted toward me like a coastal breeze shooing the chill away. He extended his arm toward a seat for me. "English Breakfast."

Great memory. He pays attention to details. He seemed sincere, but I still wondered why he had invited me. "Thank you for remembering my tea preference. And it's my pleasure to join you," I replied.

I was mesmerized by his eyes and had been staring for more than an acceptable amount of time. So, I quickly averted my eyes to my mug of tea. The moment flustered me, and I attempted to divert my embarrassment by hurriedly mentioning the weather only to produce a nod from Walt. It was a transparent attempt on my part which caused my embarrassment to increase dramatically. I worried that he might think I read more into this meeting than he had intended.

I emptied two packets of sugar into my cup and vigorously stirred. He must have sensed my uneasiness because he quickly guided the conversation to something neutral. "Since the name of this place contains the words coffee cubed, I wasn't sure they'd have tea." He took a sip of his. "Turns out they have quite a selection which was confusing to this tea lover." He chuckled.

The ice broken, I reminded myself to breathe and heard Winnie's reminder to enjoy his company.

"I first must apologize to you." Walt rested his clasped hands on the table. "When we had met at Tressa's Tuscan Cucina, you had asked me about my grandmother, and seemed so interested that I got caught up in telling my story. I forgot my manners and failed to ask about you. That was insensitive on my part and for that I am genuinely sorry."

"No need to apologize. You're correct in saying that I was very interested in your story and your grandmother's life. Her snow globe collection is so compelling. That's why I want to know her story to connect it with the globes, especially the one I purchased and any possible future purchases."

"Thank you for being so understanding. But I am genuinely interested in getting to know you. I knew I wanted to learn more about you from the moment I first saw you in the antique store."

"Really? When I clumsily knocked over the hat stand and couldn't put together a complete sentence?"

"Yes. I found you genuine, yet intriguing."

I was certain I turned several shades of blush.

Walt nodded and smiled, "So, tell me about yourself."

I inhaled, exhaled, and attempted to overcome my self-consciousness. "I grew up in Pittsburgh where my mother, stepdad, and brother still live. I've worked for a law firm here in Spring Creek for about three years."

"You came to Spring Creek for work?"

"No. I came here to be closer to Sully, my biological dad."

"My dad and I live so far from each other. It would be nice to live nearer like you and your dad."

"It was. Until he passed a few months back."

"I'm so sorry. When you had said your father had been a resident at The Willows, I assumed he had only been there to recuperate. How insensitive of me. You must still be grieving. Again, I apologize for going on about myself."

"Please don't apologize. You couldn't have known about my dad, and I was the one who encouraged you to talk about your life with Lilloise." I tried to reassure him without sounding obsessively curious regarding Lilloise.

We chatted back and forth about my life in Pittsburgh and here in Spring Creek. I tried to tell of happy times, avoided dysfunctional ones, and carefully steered clear of any mention of the snow globe travel.

During a lull in the conversation, I asked, "How is Lilloise? When we last spoke you had said she was not doing well. Has she improved at all?"

"When I had received a call earlier in the week indicating that my grandmother was not doing well, I canceled classes for the remainder of the week and drove here Wednesday morning." He cleared his throat. "She's not been conscious since I've arrived."

"I'm so sorry for you and your family." Remembering my father's last few days, I felt Walt's pain as if it were my own.

"Thank you for your compassion," he said with a nod and a tilt of his head. He then paused, inhaled, and said, "Earlier this evening, the strangest thing happened. I had stepped out of her room to retrieve snacks from the vending machine—" He smiled. "—To be honest, it was actually my unhealthy junk food dinner.

"When I'd returned, my grandmother opened her eyes, looked at me and called for Marguerite. She smiled, but only briefly. And then a deep sadness consumed her face as she slipped back into unconsciousness. It was as if she had a moment of clarity, albeit brief.

"The nurse had said it's not unusual for patients to flutter their eyes or momentarily open them, but she had never witnessed any patient speak with such clarity."

Since her moment of lucidity seemed to occur around the same time as my "travel" to Paris, I had a suspicion as to what had happened. We sat for several moments staring into our comfort drinks. I recalled my most recent trip where I had witnessed Walt as a young boy with his grandmother seemingly searching for Marguerite. I could still feel the love between them and in contrast, the profound sorrow Lilloise displayed.

I had no way of knowing what Walt was contemplating, but the look on his face spoke of bewilderment. Without divulging my knowledge of their trip, I carefully reiterated something Walt had mentioned previously.

"You had said that you once traveled with your grandmother to Paris. Do you remember much about that trip?"

"I believe I was only about ten years old." He tilted his head and glanced at the ceiling as if trying to recall. "Why do you ask?"

"I'm just trying to piece together why several times she has mentioned the name, Marguerite." I inhaled the aroma of my tea. "Seems like that might be a missing puzzle piece."

"You might be right, but keep in mind she's not been completely lucid for some time now except for the time you brought that one snow globe to her. She didn't make sense at first, but then she was peacefully calm. I will always be grateful to you for that. It was a lasting memory for me seeing her so happy."

I went on to tell him I had replaced that globe with the one of the Château de Fontainebleau. He said that he didn't remember that particular one. I was disappointed as I thought it might jog his memory of that trip with his grandmother. In an attempt to help him remember, I stretched the truth a little. Actually, I stretched it quite a lot.

"I did some research on the Château and found some interesting facts. No surprise, it is located in Fontainebleau, France." I looked to see if his beautiful eyes were following my lead. They said, I'm interested, but did not say he recalled that place. I persisted, "It's southeast of Paris and looks like a great place to visit. There's a quaint little hotel called the Hotel de Londres. And in my research, I saw a most unusual carousel with giraffes, ornate horses, a replica antique car and an airplane. It even had a small-sized hot air balloon as part of the carousel."

Walt smiled with his eyes. "That sounds charming."

"Yes. I love carousels." I sighed as it appeared the descriptions had not helped him remember that trip.

"If you ever visit me in New York, —" his face exposed pure panic. "—I'm so sorry. That was very bold of me to assume you might consider a visit."

"That's a lovely suggestion." I smiled. "I, I, I'd love to visit New York and especially take in a Broadway show." I was flattered that he actually thought about me visiting him.

His sigh revealed his relief. "I was about to tell you about this merry-go-round where you ride inside iridescent fiberglass fish while classical music accompanies the riders. It's called the Sea Glass Carousel. It's even more beautiful at night when it's illuminated."

"Sounds like New York just flew to the top of my bucket list." I smiled.

He returned my smile.

Chapter Twenty-Four

Spring Creek 2011

Saturday morning Walt texted and asked if I was free to accompany him on a shopping trip exploring Spring Creek. I texted him back explaining that there weren't many stores and asked if he would rather go to a larger town with more shop selections. He said he only needed a few things and thought he could find them all in Spring Creek. We agreed to meet in front of the coffee shop in two hours.

I quickly showered and then made a minimal breakfast of toast with strawberry jam. Some of the jam dripped off the toast, but luckily I was still in my bathrobe. The entire time from showering to toasting the bread, to eating, I contemplated what to wear. Still not sure if his invite was just because I was the only person he knew in Spring Creek or if he maybe, just maybe, enjoyed my company. I knew for sure I enjoyed his.

First, I put on a pair of jeans and a cable knit sweater but then thought that I might be too warm. I didn't trust Ronnie Dante since his forecasts were frequently incorrect, so I wasn't certain of the weather. I kept the jeans on but swapped out the sweater for a blouse. After three more outfit changes, which I discarded over the top of the chair, I went back to the boot cut jeans, tan leather ankle boots, a blue floral shirred peplum blouse, and a navy blazer. To finish the look, I inserted my pearl earrings that Sully had given me. I was always afraid of losing them, so I never wanted to wear them. But I needed reassurance from Sully, and I knew his spirit would be with me encouraging me to step out of my comfort zone.

When I arrived, only five minutes late, Walt was holding two to-go cups of coffee.

"Two sugars. Right?" His smile warmed me before I took my first sip.

He was dressed impeccably as I had expected he would be—blue jeans, a crisp white shirt, and a navy blazer.

"I should have worn my blue floral shirt!" Walt chuckled. "Then we would have matched."

I looked down at what I was wearing. I had changed so many times, I had forgotten. I looked from myself to him and back. "What's that they say about great minds?" I laughed, too.

A new bookshop had opened on one of the side streets off Main. We explored it together like two kids in a sweet shop.

"Look at this one!" he exclaimed. "And I've been looking for this travel book about the Greek Island, Sifnos. Many of the books in my collection do not include Sifnos."

In his other hand, he had a book about UNESCO World Heritage Sites.

"That looks interesting. Planning a trip to the Acropolis?" I asked.

"No. This book is a gift for a friend," Walt answered.

I wanted him to elaborate on the word friend, but he had moved on to the next table.

The salesclerk walked toward us and stopped in between. "Are you finding everything okay?" She had a scarf tied around her head and braids peeking out from under. I watched her eyebrow piercing move with her expressions.

"Yes, thank you. We're just browsing, but I've located some interesting finds."

Walt did not reply. He seemed immersed in the pile on the table in front of him.

"I'm deciding between this one which describes the childhood homes and museums of famous authors..." I showed her the front cover. "...or this one."

She didn't wait for me to show her the other one. She quickly said, "Personally, I find walking in the footsteps of famous authors fascinating. When I was in Portland, Maine, I visited Wadsworth-Longfellow's house. I could hardly breathe knowing I was walking on the same floorboards that he had once walked on. My feet were glued in place when I stood in front of his writing desk."

"This one it is, then." I placed the other book back on the table and then headed toward Walt.

He had already made it to the cashier's desk with a stack of six. "Two of these are for my father and one is for a friend." He smiled. "I didn't want you to think I was a book hoarder."

"I'd find nothing wrong with that." I nodded. *He's mentioned that friend several times. It must be someone special.*

We lunched at a little quirky café called, The Little Quirky Café. It lived up to its name. Sully and I used to have lunch there mainly on weekends. The walls were covered with glossy brightly painted items including half chairs, bicycle wheels, and broken guitars.

The menu was just as quirky. Sully and I loved the vegan options even though neither of us were vegan. But they also had beef burgers with concoctions including coleslaw and onion rings between the buns. Their soups were delicious. Each day they featured a different kind. The chicken noodle was always my favorite because the noodles were as thick as if three had been stuck together. It included some fresh herbs which I identified to be basil, rosemary, thyme, and a few others which I could not identify. The combination of herbs and thick noodles made it stand out above all others.

Walt needed to get back to The Willows, so we parted after lunch. He offered to drive me back to my apartment, but I told him I had another stop. I invited him to join Carl, Winnie, and me at Carl's favorite club in Embersville that evening, but since his dad had stayed by Lilloise's bedside all day, he wanted to spend the evening with her giving his dad a break.

I floated home re-experiencing the morning's events in my mind. I was amazed at how much we had in common. We loved books, loved the same quirky luncheon place as Sully and I had, and we both loved to travel. Walt for real and me in my dreams.

We had agreed to meet the next day for a Sunday brunch at a place near The Willows. I couldn't believe we were getting together again the next day. I allowed myself to think he liked my company, and maybe it wasn't just because I was the only person in Spring Creek he knew.

I arrived early to pick up Winnie that evening still reeling from the wonderful morning with Walt. We'd made plans to ride together so I wouldn't have to walk into the club alone. The sign was still in her front yard, but luckily there was no SOLD sticker across it. I let myself in and yelled, "Winnie, I'm early, take your time."

Her voice traveled down from upstairs. "Be down in a few."

I entered the living room and made note that all her knickknacks and family photos were still in place. *Good. It doesn't appear that she's started packing, yet.*

As I came to the photos of Jen's and Crystal's high school graduations hanging next to Winnie's granddaughter's photos, I thought about all the memories they had made in that home – Christmases, birthday celebrations, bringing home babies from the hospital. There was a beautiful picture of Winnie and Jim's wedding day and another of the whole family including their son-in-laws. It looked like they had been on vacation, and someone organized the family's color-matching outfits. I partially understood why Winnie needed to move closer to family, but hadn't she said Carl and I were like family now?

"That was taken at Sea Isle, New Jersey." Winnie came in from the hall, walked up to the photo, and touched it as if she could feel the memories. "Jim loved his cabin, but Sea Isle was my favorite place to vacation. There's nothing better than to recharge the soul with sun, sand, and sea air."

"We're only a few hours' drive away from the beach. Why are you moving so far away from that?" I hadn't intended it to sound like I was scolding her, but that was how it came out.

"Jade," she replied. Her voice softened. "I need to be near my family. I had hoped you would understand."

"You've lived in Spring Creek your whole life. You're leaving the house where you raised your girls. You're leaving life-long friends and your church family. Are you sure you've thought this through? Are you sure selling this house and moving so far away is the right decision?" I finished my speech with, "You realize you won't be able to visit Jim's grave."

Winnie did not interrupt. She just looked at me with loving, understanding eyes. "I stopped by Jim's grave before I contacted the real estate agent. I had a long talk with him. I feel in my heart that he's okay with my decision." She stroked my cheek with the back of her hand. "I won't know if it's the right or wrong decision until I take the leap."

I could feel the tears well in my eyes. She hugged me and patted my back. "You're going to be okay, Jade. Now, let's go have a drink, listen to some music, and let loose."

Winnie and I stayed for two sets and enjoyed Phoenix's band. They covered a few popular bands' songs including some country rock music, and then performed a few original ones. In between sets, Phoenix joined us at our table, bought us a round of drinks and was very amiable. I couldn't put my finger on it, but I did not get a good vibe from him. He seemed to glance around the room as if expecting someone or expecting something to happen. He was not entirely attentive to Carl. She did not seem to mind or maybe she hadn't noticed. Pessimistic Jade did, though. My distrust of relationships, especially with men, reared its ugly head.

When Phoenix excused himself to get ready for the next set, Carl told Winnie and me that she was going to ask Phoenix to move in with her. He stayed in hotels when he was performing in Embersville or in nearby towns playing gigs. She used the excuse that she thought her place would be more convenient for him. I attempted to suggest that Carl give the relationship a little more time, but Winnie's opinion outright warned Carl that it was way too soon for that type of commitment. Carl just shrugged.

Chapter Twenty-Five

Spring Creek 2011

I had only one beer the night before as I did not want to feel the effects of alcohol the next morning. I had a great night's sleep even though I was anxious to see where Walt and my friendship would go.

We met for brunch at the Park Terrace Inn. During our meal I asked if there was any change to Lilloise's health. I really wanted to know if she had gained consciousness as I was anxious to see her again. He said that she had not opened her eyes since the one incident where she had called for Marguerite.

"It must be so difficult not being able to communicate with her," I said.

"I still speak to her and reminisce. It may be my imagination, but it seems to calm her labored breathing," Walt said as he stirred his tea.

"I'm sorry I couldn't have gotten to know her. She sounds like she had a very interesting life."

"If you're not busy after brunch, we could go together to visit with her," he said, sounding like it was in the form of a question. "You won't be able to communicate with her, but my father will be there. I've told him about you, and he's anxious to meet you."

I was certain I blushed at the thought of Walt discussing me with his father.

"I'd love to meet him and see Lilloise again."

"Great." Walt smiled. "You piqued my curiosity regarding Fontainebleau, France after you had described it so lovingly. I went on the internet and found pictures of the carousel you'd mentioned." He placed his hands over his heart. "I immediately recognized it as the same one my grandmama had taken me on when we had visited. So many memories came flooding back. Mostly good ones like when we both rode that carousel and laughed and laughed. Grandmama had jumped off when it had stopped so that she could buy more ride tickets. It was so long ago, but I now remember that we rode it over and over again so that I could try out all the different animals and vehicles.

I do recall, though, there was one particular day when she was so sad. There was nothing I could do or say to console her." Walt sighed. He looked at me, but it seemed he was looking right through me all the way to Fontainebleau.

I placed my hand over his to show I understood even though he had no idea I had shared in Lilloise's moment of despair. He patted my hand as if to thank me.

Walt shook his head possibly to shake off the unhappy memory. "I want to give you a little thank you gift to show how much I appreciate your generosity and our new friendship."

It was sort of a relief that he'd defined our relationship as a "friendship." I no longer had to wonder if his intentions were more than that. And since the Nicholas fiasco, I wasn't totally sure I was ready for anything more than a friendship.

Walt pulled a small purple bag from under the table and handed it to me. It had blue and purple striped tissue paper poking from the opening like a bouquet of freshly picked lupines. Buried beneath the tissue was a beautiful porcelain carousel horse.

"Thank you for everything you have done for me and my grandmama." He sighed. His sigh sounded as if he had released weeks of worry. "You have truly been a blessing during this difficult time."

Words evaded my lips, but my heart cherished the moment with him.

After brunch, Walt followed me back to my apartment so that we would not have to take both cars to The Willows. I parked Morty and then slid into the passenger side of his Volvo. It was lovely riding in his immaculate car compared to my Morty's noisy, shaky ride.

When we arrived, I did not recognize the nurse at the front desk. I assumed Effie was not working that day. We made our way to Lilloise's room, and a slightly older version of Walt greeted us.

"It's so very nice to meet you, Mr. Milton," I shook his outstretched hand.

"Please call me Milty. Everyone does." He winked. "When I hear Mr. Milton, I think of my dad. And when I hear Walter, I think of my son." He smiled. "It can be so confusing."

Seated by Lilloise's bedside, we told him the story of how she had mentioned Marguerite several times and we asked if he knew who she was? He remembered once hearing his mother (Lilloise) and his father (Walter Milton, Sr.) arguing, and when Marguerite's name had been mentioned, his father had cursed. That was the first and only time Milty had ever heard his father use vulgar language. Lilloise's husband had said that he never wanted to hear that name ever again. Lilloise came out of the room sobbing but had slammed the door visibly angry. Milty had been so frightened that he had never asked who Marguerite was. He'd actually forgotten about it until we mentioned her name.

Milty welcomed reminiscing about his mother's life. He was very proud of her. He talked about how unusual it was for a woman at that time to graduate from college. She had earned a degree in French literature at Cedar Crest College and after graduation had taught at that same institute. She married at age twenty-nine and had Milty at age thirty. He suspected that she had put off marriage until the pressure from her father was too much and so she married the man her father had chosen.

At that time, most women stopped working when they had children, but she was so beloved at that college, they encouraged her to stay on. Milty was Lilloise's only child and had a nanny who basically raised him from infancy.

Walt and his father smiled at me and then briefly spoke to each other in French.

"I'm impressed," I said.

"We have Lilloise to thank. She insisted we learn another language, and French was her favorite. She had referred to it as her melodic love language."

As they reminisced about the many happy times, there remained a sadness in their voices. They were grieving their loss even before she was gone. I was still grieving Sully's absence. I was not sure how long it would take for the cloud to lift, but I continued to have mornings when I awoke and my eyes immediately formed pools of tears. Sometimes I would have one-sided conversations with Sully. That helped to ease the emptiness as if he were listening and at any moment would give me supportive advice.

Walt's and Milty's stories about Lilloise were incredibly intriguing. I wanted to learn more about her and especially about her early years in Paris, but most of their stories centered around her life in New York or her estate in Pennsylvania. I yearned to tell them what I knew about Marguerite but feared being thought foolish. Even I had thought myself idiotic when I had believed I was letting Zelda hypnotize me. But when I was able to view Lilloise and Marguerite in Paris without Zelda's presence, I realized the experience was unexplainable yet unquestionably real.

Milty welcomed my questions and thanked me for my interest in his mother. He said that he loved sharing his remarkable mother's life story. The resemblance between Mr. Milton and Walt was incredible. Not only in appearance, but it was clear where Walt learned manners, commitment to family, and empathy for others. I was honored to have met these incredible men and wished I could have known Lilloise when she had been aware of the world around her.

Walt drove me home, and I invited him in. "I'd love to cook dinner for you. We haven't eaten since brunch."

"I don't want to impose. I've taken up enough of your day."

"It's no imposition. You can eat here and take some back for your father. Or if you need to get back right away, I can put it in containers for you to eat with Milty."

"That is so considerate of you." He held open the car door for me. "I was probably going to go through a fast-food drive thru and pick up dinner for us or the other option would probably be eating junk food from the vending machine again." We walked up to my apartment. "I have time to eat with you, and I know my dad will be grateful if I bring him some home-cooked food."

I quickly threw together some ingredients to baste the top of the fresh salmon I luckily had in the fridge. Then placed it into the oven. In a large crockery bowl, I ripped and then tossed together pieces of romaine, red leaf lettuce, and Belgian endive. I selected the large chef's knife from the wooden block—the one Sully had treasured the most. It and the other knives had waited patiently for me to be willing to use them without him. I felt his presence as I grasped my fingers around the handle and quickly sliced through the zucchini, mushrooms, and plum tomatoes. Then I julienned a raw carrot to add to the mix. At the end I added some kalamata olives, a few walnuts, and croutons that I had made earlier from a recipe Sully had invented. I dressed the salad with virgin olive oil, fresh squeezed lemon juice, and a sprinkle of Maldon Sea Salt flakes.

"That salad looks like a work of art. I'm afraid to ask because you have everything under control, but may I help in any way?"

"You just sit and relax." I snapped the ends off some fresh green beans. "Help yourself to a glass of wine or there's beer in the fridge."

Walt selected Sauvignon Blanc from my sparse wine collection of three bottles. He reminded me of a sommelier as he uncorked it with one smooth motion as if the bottle's cork had been greased for ease of removal. He poured us both a glass and tipped his glass toward me almost in a salute, took a sip, and nodded in approval. He sat on the counter stool and observed me as if he was

218

watching a cooking show on the television. "You are like a cooking Ninja handling that knife."

I blinked away a tear and hoped he thought I had just sliced an onion.

During dinner Walt praised the meal I had prepared, "This is delicious. The infused flavors melt in my mouth and then burst with a fascinating mixture of delightful seasonings. Better than anything I've had in any of the restaurants in New York." He took another forkful, brought it up to his eye level, licked his lips, closed his eyes, and then meticulously delivered it into his waiting mouth. "Mm, mm, mm," he said as he appeared to be savoring each bite.

I could feel my chest tighten as I thought of Sully and how proud he would be of me.

"And what is this?" He moved onto one of the side dishes I had prepared. "I don't think I've ever had anything like it." Walt smacked his lips in apparent approval.

"It's a recipe handed down from my grandmother." I felt strange calling her my grandmother since I barely knew her and had only met her over long distance phone calls. But Sully had used several of her recipes from her homeland of Ghana and handed them down to me. "It basically consists of yams and red onions."

"I don't know which I like better—" He took a huge forkful of rice. "—the yams or this savory rice dish."

"It's called Jollof. It's also one of my grandmother's recipes." I filled my fork with as much rice that matched his. "It's my favorite."

Walt raised his glass. "To grandmothers…yours and mine."

"This meal is intoxicating." Walt asked, "Have you ever thought of doing this professionally?"

I did not want to explain to Walt that I nearly cry every time I cook a meal because I was still grieving Sully. And that was the main reason I stopped myself from pursuing a career in any type of food preparation or restaurant work.

So instead, I just said, "Thank you. It's one of my passions."

"Sometimes our passions are clues as to what dreams we should be chasing."

I nodded and then let his words simmer in my mind.

Chapter Twenty-Six

Spring Creek 2011

Walt remained in Spring Creek as his university was off for fall break. He enjoyed early morning hikes and had asked if I would join him sometime. I had already planned on taking Monday and Tuesday off as I was required to use my vacation days before the end of the year and I thought I would, as Winnie had put it, picture an exciting, joyful, content life. I intended to use the time to research colleges and maybe begin a job search, but spending time with Walt would fulfill the excitement part. So, I told him I could join him on Monday as that was to be the nicest weather day that week. I pushed my research to Tuesday.

Although I had only known him a short time, I found being in Walt's presence comforting—a feeling I had not experienced in a very long time. I thought I'd had that with Nicholas, but in reality, I had fantasized the relationship to be more than it actually was. After the split with Nicholas, I realized my skewed perception had allowed me to ignore the many red flags that should have shown me Nicholas' true character. I just loved being in love and therefore that was what had given me comfort rather than the actual relationship.

I suggested to Walt that we meet at the beginning of the Three Creeks Trail, but he asked if I wouldn't mind a trail which he had used during summers spent with his gram. We agreed on eight a.m., and he would pick me up at my apartment.

I was not surprised when he tapped on my door, at exactly eight o'clock. I found his punctuality refreshing and was determined to imitate his promptness. I, less than athletic Jade Fair, was actually excited to go on a hike on my day off at eight o'clock in the morning. And I could not believe it myself, but I was ready on time. What had happened to me?

When I opened the door, there stood Walt with his heart-warming smile adorning his already lovely face. I tried not to let his smile deceive me, but I liked to think it was an indication that he was genuinely happy to see me and not just his typical smile. And there was that lone dimple almost causing my knees to weaken again.

He looked handsome in his rolled-up chinos, crisp white shirt, and brown loafers exposing his bare ankles. However, I felt he was overdressed for a hike, and I was definitely underdressed in my jeans, sneakers, and plaid shirt.

"Good morning, Jade," he greeted me. I loved how he tilted his head when he spoke my name. "I'm thrilled you agreed to join me." My heart fluttered with the combination of his smile, his dimple, and the word 'thrilled.'

"Thank you for the invite," I replied. I could not say thrilled because I was unsure that I would be able to keep up with him on the hike even though my shoes were more appropriate than his. He seemed to be in excellent physical shape so maybe the difference in our shoes would not matter. I would probably be the winded one. However, I was still happy to be in his company.

"How do you feel about dogs?" he asked, holding the door for me.

This time, I tilted my head. "I uh, like them." What an unusual segway into a conversation. "Why do you ask?"

Walt grinned and extended his arm indicating he would follow me down the stairs.

At his car, he opened the passenger door and Walt's former question regarding my feelings about dogs became clear. One huge brown eye stared at me from the back seat. The other eye was shut. Perched atop its enormous head were two huge triangular ears standing at attention and a large black and white tail that beat out a tune on the back seat.

"Jade, meet Odin."

I leaned in to be greeted with a big wet kiss. "You are one beautiful pup."

"I'm so glad you like him." Walt sighed. "He's been a comfort during these tough times."

"I can see that." I scratched Odin on the top of his head as he pawed me for more. "Where have you been hiding him?"

"I usually leave him in New York at a friend's place." Walt reached in to give him a pat, too. "But this time I didn't know how long I'd be gone so I checked with the hotel, and they allowed dogs."

I reminded myself to dismiss negative thoughts. So, instead of thinking "a friend's place" meant he had a girlfriend, I envisioned that thought being washed away by a receding ocean tide. I took a breath and said, "Well, I'm pleased Odin will be joining us on our hike. Dogs have a way of lifting my spirits and making me smile."

When Walt reached in to also give Odin a pat, he was so close to me I could smell the scent of his shampoo. It was fresh but sweet. Even though it was a brisk morning, warmth climbed up my cheeks. I knew I had blushed. I hoped he would assume the red glow in my cheeks was from the chilled air.

Conversation was easy on the nearly forty-five-minute ride. He told me that he had adopted Odin from a shelter, and they had estimated he was about four years old. Walt had him for a year making him approximately five. He'd named him Odin who was a god with one eye in Norse mythology.

I told him about The Beast and my volunteer work at the shelter. He seemed impressed with my volunteerism.

Walt kept secret the location of our upcoming hike. We left the highway and traveled down a two-lane country road for several miles. I wondered if he should be away from Lilloise this long, but he said that his father insisted he take some time to spend with me. I must have had a surprised look on my face as his father had just met me. I assumed Walt saw my expression because he said, "Milty likes you. And he's a very good judge of a person's character."

I was sure I blushed, again.

After numerous cow pastures, we turned onto a narrow lane which led us up a hill to its peak and there sat a breathtaking dwelling where the property had leveled.

"My grandmother's estate." Walt made a wide gesture sweeping the expanse with both arms."

I had to tell myself to close my mouth as my jaw was suspended in awe. I was also stunned at how eerily it resembled the building I had witnessed in my Paris snow globe travel. From the corner of my eye, I could see Walt, an unwavering grin plastered across his face, obviously pleased with the secret he had just revealed to me. What he most likely had not realized was that the secret seemed to be far more complicated than he was aware.

The building was neither comparable in size nor style; however, it could only be described as a villa which resembled the same cream-colored stucco exterior with green patina door and shutters. It was massive and instead of a two-story apartment

225

building, it appeared as if a French villa had been deposited on a hilltop in upstate Pennsylvania. Scrolled in black metal above the door was the name *Matisse Estate*.

"Matisse Estate," I read aloud.

"Yes. You would have thought Grandmama would have named it Milton Estate." He chuckled. "She was the type of woman who didn't always follow the decorum of the day. And that's what I love most about her."

I recalled Lilloise mentioning Marguerite Matisse to the woman at the Fontainebleau apartment. I assumed that Matisse was Marguerite's last name. I was certain that the building was an homage to Paris and the name above the door honored Marguerite.

"She'd said that she had named the estate Matisse, because in French it means 'Free and Gentle Spirit.' And that describes her perfectly."

"My grandfather, wanting to please his wife, had this built for Grandmama." Walt smiled. "She was content here, but it always seemed like she was missing something or someone. I assumed it was my grandfather whom she had missed because he mostly stayed in the city. But as I grew older, that never made sense since their relationship had always seemed so distant even when they were together.

I would bet there was a good chance that Marguerite was the missing someone. I was about to burst holding in this

226

revelation. But to suggest this to Walt, I would have to include the whole story. And I was not ready to disclose any of it.

The beauty of the estate left me flabbergasted. However, I managed to mutter, "This…this is where you grew up?"

"I mostly lived in New York, went to boarding school in Canada, and spent summers here with Grandmama.

I paused and gawked at the gorgeous building in front of us. "Instead of a hike, can I just stand here and stare?" I understood the meaning of 'it took my breath away.' Its beauty was something I'd only seen in travel magazines.

"I thought you'd like it. We can walk through the gardens out back and there is a lovely tree-lined path that leads to the lake." He hooked the leash onto Odin. "Gram named it Béatrice Lake. She had said that she chose that name because Béatrice means one who brings joy."

She certainly could not have named it Marguerite Lake as that would have upset her husband and her father. And I also recalled Lilloise referring to her as Marguerite Béatrice Matisse. The puzzle pieces were starting to fit. *That last bit of information confirmed it. Marguerite was the someone who Lillioise wished for.*

Walt pointed to a path leading to a wooded area. "There's a stone footbridge that crosses one of the creeks which eventually feeds into the lake. We can cross there and take in the views from the other side."

We walked through an abundance of aspen trees and came to a clearing which Walt said contained thousands of daisies in the spring. He told me that the field of daisies was part of Lilloise's plan. While she wasn't a very demanding person, she had insisted on the planting of numerous daisies.

"My grandfather told me that she did not have a strong opinion about landscaping the grounds, except the daisies were non-negotiable." Walt stopped, turned his head right and then left and appeared to take in the vastness of the property as if surveying it for the first time. I assumed he was recalling childhood memories. "Grandmama had said that daisies were a symbol for soulmates. I knew she probably wasn't referring to my grandfather, but I thought perhaps she meant this place was her soulmate." Walt stopped again recalling memories I supposed.

"Are you thinking about your summers here with your grandmother?" I joined his gaze.

"Mmmm. I miss her terribly." He breathed in a cleansing breath. "She hasn't been my vibrant Grandmama for months."

We continued our walk taking in the splendor of the leaves just beginning the dance toward autumn's finest peak. The aspen trees' bright yellow ones appeared to tremble as a brief wind swept through, but they clung onto the branches defying the wind to shake them from their grasp. Walt offered his hand as we stepped over a mud puddle in the middle of the path. The warmth of his hand complimented the sun's warmth on my face. I could not have

228

imagined being more content in any one single moment. As I witnessed a solitary leaf break free and float to the ground, I felt one of my protective defensive layers, that I had so carefully constructed, also break away. The only thing that would have made this moment better is if I had Sully to confide in that I was letting someone into my life. He would have been so happy for me.

A crisp shrill of wind momentarily interrupted our solitude. It hinted of winter's approach in the not-too-distant future. The leaves now shimmied as if dancing a salsa. I shivered. Walt placed his camel-colored coat onto my shoulders and wrapped his arms around me. He pulled me close, and tenderly kissed the base of my neck. I felt completely safe and placed my head back onto his broad shoulders. I turned to face him, and his lips softly brushed mine. His kiss lingered the perfect amount of time. Not so short as to lead me to believe we were just friends, and not too long for me to feel uncomfortable. He placed his cheek next to mine. And then he whispered my name. I felt his sweet warm breath on my skin. We were silent as if time had tapped us on the shoulder to remind us to cherish that moment. I knew instantly that I would hold onto those seconds and keep them close to my heart no matter what the outcome.

Odin encircled us as if he approved. My heart fluttered like hummingbird wings. So incredibly fast it seemed to have melded into one lovely flurry.

In the safety of his arms, I released a slow, peaceful exhale. I felt secure enough to open my heart, to be vulnerable and to take a risk. I realized I had been carrying around a fear that I was unlovable, that I didn't deserve to be happy. I'd been carrying it around until it nearly destroyed any chance of happiness. The weight of that fear nearly crushed me until I found the love and true kindness of others first from Sully, then Winnie and Carl, and now from Walt.

I had experienced unconditional love and learned the importance of friendships from Sully. He had an analogy that he'd repeat to me whenever I feared vulnerability of opening up to others. 'A few skeins of yarn are just fibers strung together' he would say to me. 'But knitted together, those fibers can create a blanket that will provide warmth on the coldest darkest days.' Even as he had neared death, he had scribbled on paper for me to find those lengths of yarn.

From Winnie I learned strength and how to survive life's obstacles. Carl was a pillar of optimism. And Thomas, when I had finally let him in, even taught me about forgiveness. He opened my heart to have empathy for my mother. I realized that she was holding onto prejudices, secrets, and lies which I might never be able to understand, and she could never justify. But I knew that along with those misconceptions, she carried a world of hurt and confusion.

And from Walt, I was beginning to understand the importance of simple kindness and compassion. He indicated that merely my presence was something to celebrate.

The fear of not being worthy might always linger near, but I felt strong enough to be able to push that fear aside where it belonged. I was in the process of tearing down my old wall and building a new one to keep in good experiences, good people, and good memories and the wall would also keep that fear at bay.

These good people instilled in me that I have the power to change, and my unknown future might contain marvelous experiences. I knew at that moment that I would not just let things happen as if I had no control. I would form a plan and leave room for necessary changes. It was a scary thought that I would be the architect of my life and take responsibility for all my choices. It was a risk I was willing to take. But at that moment, risk aside, I decided to just enjoy being with Walt.

We paused on the footbridge and leaned on the stone and wooden railing. We watched a cluster of leaves trickle past. As much as I treasured that perfect moment with Walt, I knew I could not be completely content until I fully opened up to him. I knew there was the risk that Walt might end this new relationship, but I could not go forward with someone who might not accept the whole me.

"I can't go any further," I blurted.

But before I could continue, Walt must have misunderstood my intention and he said, "I'm sorry we can turn back."

"No. I can't go any further in this relationship, or friendship, or...," I hesitated. "...or whatever this is."

"I apologize," he said. "It was entirely too bold of me to think it was okay to kiss you."

"No. Not the kiss. It was lovely."

Walt shrugged. "I don't understand."

"I'm mixed-race." I challenged him with a direct line from my eyes to his. I thought he was a decent human, but I had missed so many red flags during my relationship with Nicholas, I could not assume anything. I had been so mistaken about Nicholas' character.

Walt nodded while my words hung in the air.

I guess his silence says it all. At least this time I won't be dumped via a handwritten note.

I shuffled my feet, leaned over the railing, and watched another cluster of leaves meander by. Walt's silence crushed my soul. I thought he might be different and like me, for who I was. But apparently, I misread him.

"So, I guess this is over." I could not look at him.

"What?" Walt reached for my hand.

I pulled my hand back. "Your silence says it all."

"You were waiting for me to say something?" he shook his head. "I was waiting for you because I thought you had something more to add as to why you couldn't go any further."

I quickly reviewed the last few moments concluding that we each were misunderstanding the other.

Walt continued, "Look Jade, if this is about you not being interested in exploring a relationship with me, then just say so."

"I mistook your silence for rejection." A tear slid down my cheek. "I thought it was déjà vu."

"Déjà vu?" Walt furrowed his brow.

"Yes. My fiancé, Nicholas, had abandoned me when I told him."

Walt frowned.

"My mother had withheld the information that Sully, who was mixed-race, was my father and that Thomas, who is white, was not my biological father. And Thomas was complicit in her lies." I held back tears as my mother's ability to lie with ease still stung. "The worst of it was that she was ashamed of my birthright."

Walt leaned in toward me.

"I'm still sorting out my identity. For all those years, I was raised white only to discover I descended from people from Ghana, Spain, and Europe. My mother's attitude toward me was because she was ashamed of me." I shook my head as even after all those years, I continued to make sense of who I was. "It was a lot to process and still is. I'm a mess emotionally." Another tear took the same path down my cheek.

Walt once again tucked his handkerchief into my palm. "I'm not Nicholas. He sounds like a jerk." He paused. "I can't even begin to know the hurt you've endured and what you continue to experience because of the hurt others have thrust upon you. Deception always causes damages."

"The damage goes deeper than I could have imagined." I sniffled.

"I can't take your pain away. But I do hope you'll find me to be a good listener."

I dabbed at the tears that had multiplied.

"I have a father who loves me unconditionally." He took my hands into his. "And from the sound of it, although briefly, Sully was that for you."

I gave my lungs permission to exhale a bit of apprehension.

Walt's voice remained steady, "I'd like to explore a relationship with you, Jade. We have much more to discover about each other and that excites me." He rubbed my hand with his thumb. "But you need to know that no matter what—" his tone became scarily serious, "I promise to always have a hanky in my pocket for you." His dimple deepened and I melted into his arms.

Chapter Twenty-Seven

Matisse Estate 2011

The rest of the day was magical. We walked and talked and paused for a quick kiss. Odin was patient only briefly and then pulled us along to explore the grounds.

"I'd love to bring you back here in the spring. The flowers' blooms are magnificent. I'd already told you about the daisies, but there are also hydrangea, peonies, wisteria, and rows of red, pink, and yellow roses. The property transforms into an explosion of colors."

Through his descriptions I imagined fragrances saturating the entire estate grounds. As he spoke, I could almost smell the delicate scent of lilacs giving way to hyacinth and lavender.

"I'm impressed by your knowledge of a variety of flora."

"I learned so much from Stewart, the main gardener. The one smell that transports me back in time is the smell of soil. I loved watching the gardeners turn the rich brown dirt every spring when they would clear the ground for the new plantings. Stewart had organized the plants so that something was always in bloom from May through September."

He closed his eyes, and a contented look crossed his entire face. Then as if a fond memory popped into his head, he exclaimed, "Oh! I loved when Grandmama and I would play a guessing game with the blossoms. Each of us would gather a variety of flowers or petals and with eyes closed, we would have to guess the flower by its scent only."

I listened intently as I replaced envy of his experiences with joy for him. I discovered it was much easier to choose happiness and contentment in the present moments rather than letting anger and resentment guide me.

We looped halfway around the lake, returned over the stone bridge and finished the walk back at the stucco villa. Walt pulled keys from his pocket, rattled them in front of my nose and teased, "Care to explore the inside?"

I sprinted to the door before my answer burst through my lips. "Yes!" I called back to him.

We entered through massive carved wooden double doors to an entry that can only be described as dreamlike. It was two times the size of my apartment. The two-story hallway had a marble runway-like floor with mosaics set into it every few feet and the walls scaled the perimeter up to an ornate plastered ceiling adorned with crystal candelabras. The paneled walls were lined with stained glass sconces and at the end of the hall was an expansive staircase with scrolled iron handrails.

As we walked down the paneled hall, I glanced to the left where two pocket doors were ajar just enough for me to peek inside the ornately decorated sitting room. Gilded sofas flanked an ornate marble fireplace. It seemed as if there should have been red velvet barriers protecting uncouth visitors from stepping inside and sitting on the museum-like furniture. So formal it was difficult to imagine Walt growing up here. He was mannerly, but in no way formal.

Continuing down the hall, I glanced into a parlor with a white stone fireplace so tall I could almost walk into it. The furnishings, of all shades of white and ivory, matched the draperies and carpet. There were no plastic coverings on the furnishings like I remembered from my childhood in my grandmother's living room. Since Grandma Gilda did not have air conditioning, the plastic would stick to my legs when I sat on her side chairs and had been quite painful when attempting to stand.

Further down and on the left, Walt slid open two massive pocket doors to reveal a library. We entered and he slid the doors closed. "This was one of my favorite hiding places. With the doors closed, it is a quiet retreat."

Shelves stretched from floor to ceiling housing beautiful leather-bound books. Everywhere I looked books were shelved from floor to ceiling. Many appeared as if they might be first edition collections. I could smell the aged leather and it reminded me of the hours I had spent in the Carnegie Library just four bus stops from our apartment. It was so large; I would get lost for hours just exploring. It had been a magical escape for me.

"Would you like to sit in here for a while?" Walt asked. "Your eyes are sparkling, and as if I didn't already know by our time spent in the bookstore, your grin confirms that you love books."

We sat and talked and then sat in silence taking in the splendor of the stacks. Walt interrupted the perfect moment by an even lovelier moment. He pulled several of his favorites from the collection and handed them to me. I stroked the worn leather and cracked the spines as I perused the contents. I loved the feel of the leather in my hands. A well-worn crackled spine told me they had been well read. We discussed Keats, Longfellow, and Browning. He read aloud, "To Autumn," by Keats. I absorbed every word as if it were the first time I had heard it. I firmly believed that poems were meant to be read aloud.

Walt invited me to stand on the dark wooden rolling library ladder. Then without warning he pushed me the length of the wall. I squealed like a five-year-old which sent Walt into hysterics.

"I couldn't resist," he said through his laughter. "My grandmama used to do the same to me."

"Your grandmother sounds like a wonderful person. You are so lucky to have grown up here with her."

Walt went on to describe how he never underappreciated the privilege and opportunities he'd had. His grandmother reminded him that it was his responsibility to serve and help others whenever he could. That's why he chose teaching as his profession. When he told his grandmother about students struggling to stay enrolled due to money concerns, she secretly paid each of their tuitions.

"You are the only person, besides Lilloise and me, to know that," he confided to me another of his and Lilloise's secrets. "She insisted the students never know where the money came from but would send an anonymous note asking them to pay it forward whenever they became successful."

"Since you seem to admire my grandmother's snow globes, I'd like you to see the rest of her collection."

Walt led me up the grand staircase to a room with a set of wooden double doors. In one swooping motion he opened both doors to display the most beautiful room of the estate. Overwhelmed by its sophistication, I hesitated in the doorway. He gently placed his hand on the small of my back and led me into Lilloise's bedroom. The room was effortlessly elegant without being over the top. The grand wooden cream-colored headboard complimented the carved garland swag decorating the footboard. A lacy white linen bedspread flowed over the edges of the mattress gathering onto the floor like a pool of rippled water at the base of a gentle waterfall.

Leaning against the headboard were layers of boudoir pillows made from the same lacy white linen fabric. At least

239

twelve-foot-high windows adorned with graceful sheer curtains flanked each side of the bed.

On the adjacent wall stood a dressing table with a large carved mirror mounted on the back replicating the same garland swag from the footboard and an upholstered stool also with the same carved swag. I pictured Lilloise brushing her flowing hair in front of the mirror perhaps thinking about happy times spent with her Parisian friend.

A sophisticated crystal chandelier graced the center of the ceiling surrounded by a plaster medallion which cast a brilliant sparkling glow onto the room creating an atmosphere of comfortable elegance.

A Persian rug peeked out on all sides of the bed revealing a white-on-white floral pattern.

The piece de resistance was the limestone fireplace with a mantel matching the floral swag. Atop the mantel was the remainder of Lilloise's snow globe collection. I stopped at each one and examined them. Many were from various European countries, but again, the majority were from Paris.

But on the wall across from the bed in full view hung a painting that prevented my feet from moving. It was an oil painting framed in gilded gold of the Musée du Louvre, before the glass pyramid had been added. Two women standing shoulder to shoulder faced the former palace. My eyes were glued to it.

"It's a beautiful painting. Don't you think?" Walt stood beside me. "Grandmama had commissioned it."

I nodded.

"She loved the original building and thought the glass pyramid was inconsistent with the style of the Louvre." Walt ran his fingers over the gold frame. "She was strongly opinionated about it. She felt that although Egyptian pyramids represented life after death, to her the one at the Louvre just symbolized death."

"She sounds like a very introspective woman."

"That she was. Sometimes even mysterious." Walt took my hand. "There's someone you have got to meet."

We descended the expansive staircase, proceeded down a long hall, to the kitchen. Before he opened the door he said, "You are going to love Hilde."

Walt went on to explain that Hilde oversaw the kitchen staff and general household maintenance, while her husband, Stewart maintained the landscaping and staff. They had emigrated from Germany nearly forty years ago. Those were their first jobs, and they'd been with the family ever since. They lived on the grounds in a cottage at the edge of the property.

When we entered the kitchen, a petite rounded woman with her back to us, stood in front of an eight-burner stove. She had thick salt-and-pepper hair which was wound into a snug bun perched on top of her head. She stood on her toes and stirred a gigantic cast iron pot on one of the burners. The scent emanating from the pot smelled like a welcoming hug.

"Hilde!" Walt ran to her and hugged her with an embrace that lifted her off the floor.

"Can it be my little Wally?" She gently pinched Walt's cheeks.

I smiled when she'd called him 'little' as his height towered over her.

"Mmmm. You smell like chicken soup." Walt teased.

"Of course, I do. It's the perfume of queens." She returned his quip with her own.

"Hilde, I'd like you to meet my friend, Jade." Walt motioned for me to join them.

"Friend?" Hilde winked. "Anyone who is a friend of Wally's is a friend of mine." Although she had lived in the States for almost forty years, her accent hinted of her original language.

"It has been too long since my last visit. And I'm sorry for that." Walt placed his hand on my elbow guiding me closer to him.

"No apologizing. Remember. Always do better." Her smile shone with apparent love for him. "Now have a seat, you two. The soup is ready."

"We might as well have a bowl." Walt nodded toward the wooden table and chairs residing in a cozy nook flanked by multi-paned windows. "Hilde will insist until we do, and I guarantee you will not regret it. She really is the queen of the kitchen."

Hilde served us each a bowl of piping hot chicken noodle soup as Odin patiently waited at her feet. "I haven't forgotten about you. Don't worry. I'll get your bowls."

As she filled Odin's bowls with water and dog food, she asked Walt, "How is Lilloise? I want to hear all about her. Sometimes the news does not reach us here."

Walt went on to describe Lilloise's condition and that he feared she would not be with us for very long. He added that even though she had lived a very long life, he was still not ready to let her go.

Hilde patted Walt's shoulder. "We never are ready to let them go." She shook her head.

She listened intently while cleaning and chopping vegetables. Then she told stories of Walt as a boy growing up. How he had loved to slide down the banister even though it had been forbidden.

As she recounted numerous stories about Walt, I pictured him as a ten-year-old running through the massive hall and sliding as if he were sliding into home plate and then squealing with delight. She described him as a sweet boy but with a devilish side, too. He loved to play tricks on Stewart hiding toy cars throughout the landscaping.

When it was time for us to leave, Hilde patted Walt's cheeks and said, "Don't be a stranger. We miss seeing you. And be sure you bring Jade." She threw a wink to me. "You're welcome even without Wally."

"Where's Stewart?" Walt asked. "I'd like to say hi before we go,"

"He took some equipment to be repaired. He'll be so disappointed he missed you."

"Please tell him hello for me."

I thanked her for the wonderful soup, and several hugs later, we left through the massive front doors each with a to-go container of soup. On the circle driveway, I turned to take in a last lingering look at the beautiful villa. That was when I spied Walt pulling a miniature toy car from his pocket and tossing it into one of the planters to the left of the doorway. He must have realized I had caught him because he smirked, placed his finger to his lips, and then mouthed to me, "our little secret."

Chapter Twenty-Eight

Spring Creek 2011

On the drive back to Spring Creek, A police car's flashing red lights prompted Walt to immediately pull the car over to the berm of the road. Walt was extremely polite and respectful using "yes sir" and "no sir" when addressing the officer's questions. He examined Walt's driver's license and asked where we were headed. Walt told him we were on our way to visit his grandmother in The Willows Nursing Facility near Spring Creek.

The officer returned the ID. "I'll give you a warning this time, but next time make sure you come to a complete stop at a stop sign." He nodded and said, "Have a nice day."

"Yes, sir. Thank you, officer." Walt sighed. "You do the same."

For the next few minutes, I stared out the side window.

"Sorry about that." Walt broke the silence. "You seemed a little shaken. Did that unnerve you?"

I shook my head. "It just reminded me of an incident I'd experienced with Sully. It had occurred quite differently though."

"I'm listening." Walt came to a complete stop at the next stop sign.

I told him about the time when Sully had been driving, and I had been a passenger. We were pulled over by similar flashing red lights and the officer gave no indication as to the reason. He asked me if I was okay. Not once, but three times. It seemed like he was searching my face and his tone implied that he thought I was in distress. He asked for Sully's license, walked back to his squad car, eventually returned, and handed Sully back his license. Still no explanation and then he drove away.

I felt guilty that my father had experienced racism his whole life. I was only spared because of my light skin as well as my mother's lies.

I went on to tell Walt about my first meeting with Sully. It had been at the restaurant where he was the head chef. When he approached my table, I instantly realized that my mother had not just disliked me, she had been ashamed of me. It smacked me like a karate kick straight to my gut. The hurt had gone deep into places I had not known existed. She was such a hypocrite. She'd had an intimate relationship with a mixed-race man but could not accept her own daughter.

When I explained to Sully the toxic relationship I had with my mother, he could not have been more empathetic. He said he was sorry he could not have been there to support me. Sully asked if he could hug me and when I had said yes, his arms gently surrounded me, comforting me in a way I had never experienced. It felt like I was home, a home I had always longed for, a home I had hoped to find one day, and indeed I did when I met Sully. When I first looked into his eyes, it was like looking in a mirror at my own reflection.

We talked for hours, and he told me he was thrilled when I had contacted him. He had no other children and confessed that he loved having a daughter before he had ever met me in person.

At that point in my story, Walt smiled and said, "That's so touching. Please tell me more."

I explained to Walt how excited I had been to tell Nicholas about meeting my father. I called my fiancé as soon as I had gotten to my hotel room. I talked on and on about Sully and had no idea there might be an issue. I stayed in Spring Creek one week and then returned to Pittsburgh. When I entered our apartment, I found that Nicholas had moved out. It seemed that he was okay with having Black and Brown friends, but not a mixed-race fiancé. So, he left me a note. A stinking note. That's all I had meant to him. A stinking piece of paper. I thought he loved me more than he really had. He was a hypocrite just like my mother. She had long-time friendships with Black and Brown friends. Friendships were okay, but a mixed-race daughter was unacceptable to her.

I gasped at breath as the reliving of the relationship with my mother and Nicholas triggered angst that I had until that point been able to mostly squash. Retelling the events to Walt made me realize how alike Sully and I were. Not just in looks, but characteristics and mannerisms. Since my mother wanted to erase Sully from her life, my mere presence reminded her of him, and she hated me for that.

Odin nudged his head between the seats and nuzzled my arm. I stroked his head, and he pressed his chilly nose into my palm. He warmed my heart with that cold nose, giving me strength to continue.

I explained to Walt that without hesitating, Sully had invited me to join him in Spring Creek. So, I moved, without telling my mom, brother, or stepdad. I never regretted it because I got to know my dad, and no one could take that precious time away from me, ever.

I went on to explain how Sully's health had deteriorated, and it was painful to watch because eventually Sully couldn't hold a spatula let alone knives. That was all I had left of him—a few memories, a few photographs, and his professional knife set.

Walt asked to hear one of my fondest memories of Sully. I told him about how well we worked together in the kitchen and when he had an evening off, we would have the popcorn challenge where we would flavor the popcorn in various ways and were obligated to at least try it.

I smiled remembering those happy times which sent a peacefulness through me. Walt's silence allowed me to enjoy the memory. He smiled and nodded. I wondered if it reminded him of fond memories he'd had with Lilloise.

"But the one remembrance I hold most dear occurred on a Tuesday in November. We went to the polls together and voted for the forty-fourth United States Presidential candidate, Barack Obama. When Sully exited the voting booth, his shoulders were high and back. He appeared inches taller than when he had gone in. Pride streamed from the tears flowing down his face surrounding his biggest smile."

"Is there something you miss most about him?" Walt asked.

"It would have to be his laugh. It was infectious." I nodded. "Once, we had gone to a self-serve car wash and had run out of quarters. We drove all the way to his apartment with suds flying off his car. We laughed so hard that at one point he had to pull over because he couldn't see to drive with tears of laughter filling his eyes."

"I wish I could have met him." Walt glanced at me.

"That would have been sweet." I scrolled through my phone. "If you'd like, I can play a short video I have of him, and you can hear his voice."

"Let's hear it." Walt smiled.

I played the video of Sully explaining the proper way to froth egg whites. We listened, and then I pressed play a second time just to hear his voice again.

With each story that Walt coaxed from my memory, I felt anxiety leave my body. Walt knew how to shift my focus so that I did not dwell on the hurtful parts of my past which helped me to realize that I had many more happy moments than I had ever admitted. His hopefulness and enthusiasm for life's sweetest moments were like a warm hug to my soul.

When we arrived at my apartment, Odin had curled up asleep on the backseat. Walt walked me to my door, brushed my hair aside, and caressed my neck. His lips then found mine. He drew his head back, but I leaned in and took another kiss. I did not want the moment to end. His eyes met mine and he smiled. He pulled me closer, and I placed my head on his chest. I was filled with contentment as anxiety drained from my inner core. At that beautiful moment I made a conscious decision to shift my perspective. I was worthy of love. My life was in my control. And I would choose to look toward a hopeful future filled with love and friendships.

"I didn't realize a walk with you was more like walking and stopping to sniff every few feet." I tugged on Odin's leash. "Come on, boy. It'll take us all day to get to the park and back."

I had offered to take Odin on a walk the next day after our glorious hike at the estate. Walt wanted to be by Lilloise's side at the nursing home all day. With my offer he did not have to leave.

Odin and I finally made it to the statue of Bridget Jean Collins aka Jean Kerr, and he decided to also anoint it along with the bronze daisies surrounding her feet. *For as backwards as Spring Creek seems to be, they honored a woman author. Credits to Spring Creek!*

We walked past the fountain, and I strained to keep him from jumping in. I was surprised to see water still cascading from the several layers. I paused to enjoy the sounds of the water first trickling from the smaller top layer, cascading from the next two, and then splashing to the bottom pond-like circle. It was usually turned off by now in preparation for winter, but we were lucky it was not.

We walked and stopped and walked and stopped through the park and finally made it to the pond. A flock of Canada geese, who had not yet migrated south, honked as if they were warning us of winter looming near. Odin barked at them and tried to chase the birds. In doing so, he nearly pulled me to the ground. In my attempt to stay upright, I twisted my ankle and had to hobble to the nearest bench. I sat to give my ankle a rest while Odin laid his head on my lap. He wagged his tail incessantly and licked my hand. I ruffled the fur on top of his head. "I'm glad you like me." I leaned over and kissed his snout. "I'm growing close to your Walt, and it means a lot that you've accepted me."

While I rested my ankle we sat, and people watched. A lady in heels click clicked by in a hurry, probably late for work, maybe taking a shortcut through the park. I related to her lateness. A man with two toddlers in tow walked by. They were dressed alike and similar in size. I guessed they were twins. He was in a suit and probably headed to daycare and then to work. One of the toddlers tried to break free calling, "doggy, doggy." The man tightened his grip and moved on. Each time someone passed by, Odin wagged his tail as if it were helicopter blades preparing to take off. He pranced from paw to paw. When no one stopped, he looked up at me as if to ask, "Why didn't they stop?" I gave him a conciliatory pat and said, "Maybe next time. The world's a busy place."

After a brief rest, we headed back to the hotel. I let Odin into Walt's room and watched him curl up on the bed. I refreshed his water and gave him a cup of dog food. Before I left, I patted him on his head and bent over to give him a quick kiss. He reached up and replied with a slobbery thank you, then laid his head back down with a huge sigh. I supposed the walk made him tired. "I get it. I could use a nap, too."

On my way to the nursing home, I grabbed lunch for Walt and his dad at The Little Quirky Café as I knew they would probably eat something unhealthy from the vending machine.

When I entered Lilloise's room, they were sitting on either side of her bed.

"I brought you some lunch." I set the bags onto a nearby counter.

"Thank you, Jade." Milty smiled. "That was so thoughtful."

"Thank you." Walt said, averting his eyes from me. "And thank you for taking care of Odin."

I stood beside Walt and placed my hand on his shoulder, but he still did not look at me. I got the sense that maybe he wanted to be alone with Lilloise and his dad, so I excused myself. Milty walked me to the door and again thanked me. Walt stayed seated. I knew he was already mourning the inevitable loss of his beloved grandmother, but it was so out of character for him to be rude in ignoring me.

On the drive home, I reviewed every detail leading up to the abrupt change in his personality. I knew I had not imagined the connection we had made during our hike at the estate. I questioned my memory. Maybe reality was different than what I remembered. Or maybe I had shared more than he could handle. Had I pushed too much of myself into his life by offering to take care of Odin?

I replayed our conversation on the ride from the estate back to Spring Creek. I knew I had not imagined our connection at my apartment door. Maybe, just maybe he'd had time to think about all that I had told him. My complicated life might have been too much for him to process. A pain shot through my stomach and traveled to my heart. Maybe he was no better than my mother or Nicholas.

Chapter Twenty-Nine

Spring Creek 2011

When I returned to work on Wednesday, Winnie and Carl were standing like sentries outside my cubicle walls. I was sure they were anxious to know how brunch went on Sunday. It was nice to have friends interested in my life.

"So, spill," Carl didn't even wait for me to take off my coat.

Carl squeezed into my cubical and perched herself on my desk while Winnie rolled a chair closer to my cubical opening. "We've been bursting with curiosity."

"I couldn't tell," I teased.

"We want every detail, young lady." Winnie waggled her finger at me.

"It was nice." I smiled.

"Oh no. We want more than it was nice." Carl used air quotes around the words 'it was nice.'

I glanced around the office to make sure Jessica-big-ears was not anywhere nearby. I described how lovely brunch had been on Sunday and how comfortable I had been in Walt's company. I recounted the hike we had taken with Odin at the estate on Monday including the walk around the lake (carefully leaving out the intimate kiss.) I described the vibrant fall colors of the trees, and then explained how the villa's luscious interior was both lavish and welcoming. I told them that it felt like I had been transported to a villa in France.

"You were with him Sunday and Monday?" Winnie clapped. "This sounds like the relationship is getting serious."

"Wait. Whose estate?" Carl asked.

"Walt's grandmother's estate," Winnie said impatiently. "Let her finish."

It was like I was back in school giving a report in front of the class, except I was thoroughly enjoying it. I went on to describe the adventure of exploring inside the rooms of the villa and the delight of meeting the charming Hilde who had conveyed stories of Walt's childhood. They were not only fun to listen to but also gave me a sneak peek into what had produced the man he had become. And when I could no longer restrain myself, I revealed the part that had encircled my heart. I lowered my voice to barely a whisper and revealed the highlights of the kiss.

Carl placed her hands over her heart, closed her eyes, and grinned.

Winnie hugged me. "I'm so happy for you." She placed a kiss on each of my cheeks. "You deserve it."

Then I told them how I had bonded with Odin on Tuesday during our time at the park. I cautiously omitted my fearful thought that Walt may have changed his mind about me. I was hard enough on myself, and I did not need Winnie's advice telling me I was being negative.

Exhilarated, but exhausted talking about myself, I focused the conversation on them. I asked, "So, how was both of your weekends?"

Then Winnie delivered the news I had been dreading. She had an offer on her house. It was a sound bid, and it appeared that the sale would go through. I wanted to be happy for her, but I already imagined my loss.

"We'll just have to plan road trips." Carly's positive response to the news that our friend would soon be far from our everyday lives was typical Carl. "And we can always connect via texts and Zoom calls."

"This place just won't be the same," my voice cracked.

Jessica turtle-walked by us several times, her hair tucked behind her ears. So, we had to table the conversation because Winnie had not given her two-weeks' notice and was waiting until the sale was finalized.

Winnie's news that she would soon be moving away combined with my worry that Walt had ignored me the day before, caused my stomach to flip flop with nervousness. I could barely concentrate as my mind went over every detail of each moment with Walt. I tried to contain myself, but my worry won out. I texted him.

How is Lilloise?

Second Text:

I had a lovely time on Sunday and Monday. I loved taking care of Odin,too. I'd like to take you to the restaurant where Sully worked. Any chance you're available?

● ● ●

Then the dots went away. And then they returned.

● ● ●

Then the dots went away, again. And they did not return.

Maybe he's busy with Lilloise or his father. I tried to reassure myself.

As the hours ticked on, my pessimistic side initiated the chain of worry again. Thoughts popped into my head like popping corn that could not be controlled once the oil heated. Notions like, he did not like my kiss, or he thought about my past and did not want to be involved with a woman who was emotionally messed up. Those ideas competed to increase my anxiety. I could not suppress the ugly thought that he might have been another Nicholas. My head automatically slumped to my desk.

"Napping, huh?" Carl's voice startled me from my thoughts. "Too much Walt loving?"

I'm sure my face was visibly distraught, because when I looked at Carl, she stopped teasing and immediately put her arm around my shoulder. "What happened?"

"I texted Walt and he didn't respond." Saying it out loud, I heard the foolishness of my thoughts.

"Holy shit!" Carl's comforting hug switched to a tap on my head. "I thought someone had died."

"I'm being silly, I know," I straightened the pile of papers on my desk. "It's just that I like him. I like him so much."

"That's apparent." She crossed her arms. "But I know what you are doing, girly. You're letting a past hurt cloud your judgement. Walt's a good guy."

"I know. You're right." I took a deep breath to try to calm my fears and nerves. "I'm trying, but I can't change overnight."

The worry started emerging again near the end of my workday when I still had not heard from him. Even though Winnie and Carl both agreed that I should not text him again until I had heard from him, I could not help myself.

Hi! Everything okay? Let me know if there's anything I can do to help especially with Lilloise.

I hate those dots. They said, "Wait please, I'm responding." But to me they were torture. Then the dots went away. And once again, quickly returned.

Then the dots went away, again. And they did not return.

Chapter Thirty

Spring Creek 2011

As I approached my apartment, I noticed an all too familiar Land Rover parked in front. Butterflies. No. More like moths began an unpleasant dance in my stomach. The driver's side door opened, and my fear was confirmed. It was Nicholas.

"Hi Babe!" he approached with outstretched arms holding a bouquet of red roses in one hand.

I took a step back.

"I'm here to beg for forgiveness." He placed his hands together as if praying.

I took a moment to glance around for cameras because I was sure I was being punked. This jerk couldn't be serious.

"I drove all this way. Aren't you going to give me a hug and invite me in?" Without warning he stepped forward and embraced me. I stiffened.

A small group of teens walked by. "Aww," a tall blonde, one with braids, and a shorter brunette said in unison. And then they sang in harmony, "roses."

I inhaled a deep breath and forced out a few words, "Let's go inside." I did not want to confront him on the sidewalk.

"Whatever you say, Babe." He handed me the roses. "But please accept these."

I shuddered at the way he nonchalantly repeated the word 'Babe' as if we'd had no negative past. Did he assume I had forgiven him? Did he think I had been patiently waiting for this day? He nearly shoved the roses in my hand. Hesitantly, I took the bouquet as it seemed his persistence won.

Nicholas reached into his car and pulled out an overnight bag.

"Leave that in the car." My voice raised an octave. "This won't take long."

But before we entered the house, I noticed Nicholas had not put his bag back in the car. I turned to tell him again to leave the bag and that was when I was pretty sure I spied a blue Volvo coming down the street. It slowed as it passed by and then drove away.

Inside my apartment, Nicholas again approached for another hug. I backed away and attempted to set him straight, "I'm sorry you drove all this way. But you need to turn around and drive on back." I glanced at his bag. "I'm not getting back together with you. And you are definitely not staying here."

"Look, Jade." He took the flowers from me and laid them on the counter. Then he held my hands. "I thought we reconnected when you were in Pittsburgh. Didn't we? And I'm willing to do anything to get you back."

"I apologize if I gave you the wrong impression. But, have you noticed, I'm still mixed-race," I snatched my hands away. "That hasn't changed."

"But I have," he said. "I know how wrong I was."

"I'm happy for you that you've acknowledged your ignorance." I turned from him and stood next to the table where Sully's pottery waited for me. I touched it for strength. "But I no longer love you."

"I did not see that coming," he said, shock overtaking his puppy-dog expression.

"You thought after the hurt you had caused and after years of not hearing from you that I'd still pine for you?"

"I drove all this way and spent the day exploring the town that had seized my Jade." He placed his hands on my shoulders. "I wanted to get to know the place that has captivated your heart and kept you away from me."

I shrugged his hands off my shoulders and turned to face him. As I studied his face, I saw sadness and a bit of remorse. I felt sorry for him. He may have changed, but so had I. I knew what I wanted, and a life with Nicholas was not part of it.

He caught me off guard when he handed me a small velvet box. "Please take this and tell me you'll reconsider."

"Nicholas, please sit down." I directed him to the couch. I placed the box into his hands and curled his fingers around it. "I'm sorry. But I've changed. I'm excited about my future, and I realized I can decide where that future may take me."

It was difficult at first, but then I explained that what I had needed a few years ago, had changed. He hinted that he was beginning to understand, and then we reminisced about the past good times. Since he had been the person I was engaged to marry, I did not take lightly my decision to not reunite. He cried. And then I cried, but it was ultimately cleansing. Finally, there was face-to-face closure, and he understood that we were both better off apart.

"You may have been my first true love, and I was heartbroken when you broke up with me, but in the end, you gave me my freedom. And for that I am eternally grateful." My words were genuine, and I hoped he could sense that.

He told me about the several failed relationships he'd had since our split and said that none compared to what we'd had. I felt sorry for him and his epiphany that he still had feelings for me. I told him that I hoped he could find strength in himself, friends for support, and the peacefulness that I had recently discovered. We talked well into the evening. I packed him a few containers of food for the road and when he left, I was more than certain I had chosen the right path.

Chapter Thirty-One

Spring Creek 2011

The next day I again texted Walt. No three dots, just silence. At lunchtime, I called his cell. No answer. I left a message that I really wanted to see him and asked if he could call me as soon as possible. No reply.

So, after work, I drove to The Willows and spied his car in the lot. I went in and was greeted by Effie. I asked her if she could tell me of Lilloise's condition. She said that Lilloise was still not responding. She estimated that Walt's grandmother would leave us in the next few days. Effie was on her dinner break and asked if I'd like to join her and Phillip in their break room. Liz was on maternity leave. She'd not yet had the baby, but her blood pressure had spiked and her doctor had put her on bed rest.

I walked down the hall to the vending machines to purchase something to tide me over until I could get a proper dinner. As I reached in for the bag of pretzels, I heard Walt's voice. Immediately, my heart pulsed several quick beats. I peeked around the corner and saw Walt in conversation with a nurse. Before I could pull my head back around, he saw me.

"Jade?" he looked visibly upset. "What are you doing here?"

"I was just visiting with Effie," I said. Which was not a total lie. Even though my initial intent was to confront Walt, technically I was visiting with Effie.

"Oh," I detected what I hoped was a bit of disappointment in his tone.

"How are you?" I asked. "How is Lilloise?"

"She's not well," he sighed. "They think it's a matter of days."

"I'm so sorry," I said. "Is there anything I can do?"

He shook his head.

"Please let me know if you think of something, anything I can do to help." I so wanted to ask him why he had not replied to any of my texts or phone messages, but I knew he was distraught, and it was not about me.

"I'd better get back in there," he said. He started down the hall, stopped, and then turned to face me. "Oh, congratulations."

"What?" I scrunched my face as if I had devoured a basket of lemons.

"Congratulations to you and Nicholas."

"Excuse me?" My voice increased three octaves.

"Yesterday, I stopped in the coffee shop and there was a guy in front of me bragging to the barista that he was there to set a date to be married. The barista gasped when he showed her something. I was quite a bit taller and so I glanced over his shoulder. When I saw what he was holding, I understood her reaction. The diamond ring in a deep red velvet box had to have been at least two carats. They went on to discuss, I'm not sure what because at that point I was only half listening until he'd said "Jade. Jade Fair."

I listened intently to what he was saying and attempted to make sense of it.

Walt stammered, "Con—congrats to you and Nicholas on your engagement."

I immediately pieced together the confusing puzzle. It was clear that Walt had made inaccurate assumptions.

"Whatever you saw and heard, it's not true." I placed my hands firmly on my hips. "Is that why you haven't responded to me?"

"I, I, I," he mumbled. "But I saw…"

"Let me stop you right there, Mr. Walter Milton, III" I took a deep breath. "Did you drive by my apartment yesterday?"

He nodded.

"What you saw was Nicholas thinking an apology and a dozen roses would be enough to get me to return to him." I chuckled. "He was sorely mistaken, and I'm sorry you misinterpreted what your eyes and ears had revealed to you."

"But he had an overnight bag."

266

"Well, I do love flowers, so I kept the roses." I stepped closer. "I sent Nicholas and his overnight bag away. But not until I was certain that he understood that we were never, under any circumstances going to be a couple ever again."

"I didn't want to come between you and him." Walt sighed. "I only want you to be happy, and if that means me stepping aside, I will, without question, not stand in your way."

"I have someone special in my life and I don't want to mess that up." I winked. "Those heartaches I had experienced before I met you were gifts that pointed me toward you. They revealed to me what I did not want in my life." I smiled remembering Winnie's inspiring words.

Walt embraced me and I gladly welcomed it. We promised to always talk things out with each other and never assume anything.

"Now tell me what I can do for you, your father, and Lilloise." I opened my arms to see if he would welcome a hug.

"I'd be grateful if you'd sit with me by Lilloise's bedside. Just knowing you are by my side to support me would be more than enough."

We walked hand-in-hand to Lilloise's room. When we entered her room, Milty had her hand pressed to his cheek. He noticed us stopped in the doorway. He stood and walked toward me. "So nice to see you again, Jade." He reached out and gently hugged me.

"Jade's going to stay here with me," Walt spoke to his father. "Why don't you go back to the hotel and get some rest? You've been here since last night and all of today."

"Thanks, son." He nodded in agreement. "I could also use a quick shower. I'll take care of Odin and then be back in a few hours."

Walt and I sat beside Lilloise's bed. He took her hand, stroked it, and gently kissed it. I placed my head on his shoulder. The love he had for her was still as strong as that which I had witnessed when he was a boy in Paris.

"I only wish I could bring her a bit of comfort like she unselfishly provided me," he said.

I spied the snow globe next to her bed and decided to step out of my comfort zone. "Walt. Do you trust me?"

"Of course," he whispered. He lifted my chin from his shoulder. "I trust you, implicitly." He gently kissed my forehead.

I reached for the snow globe. Placed it in Lilloise's hands, reached for Walt's hands and placed mine around both of theirs. I gently rocked the snow globe back and forth.

SNOW GLOBE TRAVELER

****

Paris, France 1927
In front of the Louvre Museum

Lilloise, Walt, and I witnessed a young woman cradled by a woman who seemed to be her mother. Lilloise stood between Walt and me squeezing our hands as if she was desperate to not let go. Then she brought Walt's hand to her lips and kissed it. She dropped our hands and shuffled toward the two women. Her nearly one hundred-year-old shoulders were slumped, and her feet barely left the ground. The struggle to walk was apparent, but as she got closer to the two ladies her posture straightened and she picked up her pace. Her voice was barely audible as she called, "Marguerite." She called louder, "My Marguerite."

Marguerite lifted her head and her sobbing stopped.

With each step Lilloise's walk became less strained and as she neared Marguerite, she appeared to be her younger self. Marguerite ran to her, and they embraced.

I looked at Walt and he looked like I'm sure I had looked on my first snow globe trip, more than just confused. I squeezed his hand and mouthed, "Trust me."

Lilloise turned, faced us, blew a kiss, and said, "Thank you."

I returned a kiss through the air, my voice broke, and I replied, "We love you."

And we were back in Room 110 at The Willows. Walt looked from me to his grandmother and back to me. I supposed he was attempting to process what had just occurred.

"I'm not sure if I can explain it to you as I don't fully understand myself." I placed the snow globe back on the table. "I am sure of one thing, though. There were no coincidences between the snow globes and my meeting you. Lilloise needed to find happiness and so did I."

He nodded.

Lilloise stirred. Walt and I each took one of her hands. Her eyes remained closed, but she smiled and took her final breath.

I whispered, "We will miss you…Free and Gentle Spirit."

EPILOGUE

Pittsburgh 2012

I no longer hated Thursdays. Even though two people whom I terribly missed and ardently loved had departed the earth, I was certain that their spirits remained. In the days after Lilloise joined Marguerite, Walt leaned on me for emotional support. He understood my connection to Lilloise and Marguerite, and that provided him immense comfort. I was pleased to have been there for him. Entering into a relationship with Walt was scary, but I was determined to listen to my heart and push previous fears aside.

After he returned to New York, I gave my two-weeks' notice. I returned to Pittsburgh to help support Thomas in Mom's recovery and possibly bridge the divide between him and Will. Carnegie, a small community not too far from Thomas and Evie's apartment, had a blossoming foodie scene. I acquired a job in a restaurant and planned to follow in Sully's footsteps by working my way up learning the entire business.

Carl made the trek to Pittsburgh with me and got a job as a bartender in the same restaurant. All she would say about Phoenix was that the relationship "crashed and burned." She said that instead of a Phoenix rising from the ashes, she was a songbird soaring to a more fulfilling life.

Winnie moved to Ohio and was quite content getting to interact with her grandchildren daily instead of a few times a year. Since she was only a few hours' drive from Pittsburgh, Carl and I made trips to see her as often as we were able.

In the months that followed, Walt and I visited each other frequently. He came to Pittsburgh during his breaks from teaching and I either visited him in New York or at Matisse Estate which he had inherited from Lilloise. In her Last Will and Testament, she had stated that the name of the estate and the name of the lake was to remain and that the daisies were to be maintained. Walt and I understood her wishes when we found a note in Lilloise's desk at the estate which explained that the name Marguerite in French meant daisy.

Each time I visited the villa, Hilde taught me Walt's favorite recipes from his childhood. She and I discussed writing a cookbook together combining her cultural recipes along with the ones I had inherited from Sully. Walt and Stewart were our taste testers and they both agreed that the cookbook had the potential to actually develop from a wish into a reality.

As a gift, Walt presented me with two airline tickets to London. He said that it was time I met my grandparents, and he would gladly travel with me. I was excited to explore those branches of my family tree. My grandfather, originally from England and my grandmother, originally from Ghana, had lived in Brooklyn, New York early on in their marriage and that was where

272

Sully had been born. When Sully was twelve, they had moved back to London where they had originally met during their university years. Sully had returned to New York for college and decided to make the United States his permanent residence.

Walt also gifted me the snow globe of the Louvre. He said, "I believe Lilloise would have wanted you to have this."

I told him that I no longer needed it. I had relied on it to learn about friendship, family, and love and I had found all three. We agreed to keep it at the estate alongside the others. I never had the desire to travel again via a snow globe. My wish was to live in the present and see Paris and the world in person.

I no longer identified myself as a pessimist. However, I did not quite transform totally into an optimist either because I still had a few recurring pessimistic tendencies. Carl firmly believed that I was a recovering pessimist. I enthusiastically agreed.

V.M. BRENDEL

AUTHOR'S NOTE

The idea of *Snow Globe Traveler* was initially born when I was seemingly cemented to a spot in a store standing in front of a shelf of snow globes. I was mesmerized by the various types of orbs from carousel horses to scenes of cities I had yet to visit. I shook one after the other and the idea appeared as I watched the artificial snow drift and accumulate at the base. I thought about the places of my dreams and my bucket list of travel destinations until that point had mostly not been checked off.

Fast forward a few years. The idea continued to crop up at unexpected times while I worked on an unrelated story. I left it to simmer on a back burner until Jade spoke to me, and then I knew I needed to tell her story.

Historic license was utilized when mentioning The Sea Glass Carousel located in Battery Park in New York City. Its opening date was August 2015. I wanted to include it in Jade's story because it is one of my favorite things to do when I visit New York City.

ACKNOWLEDGEMENTS

I would like to thank my walking partner, Margaret Tarentino. After hiking on wooded trails, we stopped at our favorite tea shop, The Steeping Leaf, where we indulged in scones, smoothies, vegan wraps, and of course various teas and then edited a very rough draft of *Snow Globe Traveler*. I am grateful for her support, enthusiasm, and friendship.

I would also like to thank my daughter, Shannon Paul, and my son-in-law, Aaron Paul, for their invaluable editing. They took time out of their busy lives to read the entire manuscript and provide significant critiques. (Shannon read it twice and Aaron stayed up past midnight to finish reading.) Frequently, I relied on them via extra FaceTime calls to be able to get their opinions during what seemed like unending edits. Their contributions enabled me to develop a clearer accounting of Jade's story. I am beyond indebted to them for their vital observations, analyses, and critiques.

I must give credit to the Second Saturday Writers' Group for their critiques, guidance, and inspiration. Susan Kimmel

Wright, a member of the group and author of *Mabel*, a cozy mystery series, was not only a role model, but also my indispensable cheerleader. Her encouragement sustained me and helped me over hurdles which might have blocked me from moving toward the finish line.

Kika Wright, nonprofit administrator and anti-racism educator, completed a sensitivity read of *Snow Globe Traveler* and provided a valuable and insightful critique.

And finally, I am forever grateful for the support of my husband, Ray. He lovingly supported me, enabling me to avoid going down self-discouraging paths. He understood the many hours I needed to write and edit my manuscript and never questioned why I sometimes talked aloud to myself. He was one of my readers when I was editing an early draft, and he provided valuable insights distinctive from the other readers. I would have struggled to complete *Snow Globe Traveler* without his love and encouragement. I consider myself extremely lucky to have a wonderfully understanding husband.

About the Author

Valerie Brendel, a retired first-grade teacher, found a love of words long before teaching children to read. Early on, she would collect words in her head or scribble them in a notebook or on any available piece of paper. She saved the ones that evoked emotions, eventually composing sentences or journal entries with them, and ultimately converting them into stories. Her excitement toward writing first surfaced when a poem of hers was published in a seventh-grade yearbook.

Working, going back to college as an adult, and raising two children absorbed most of her time. Writing had always been a hobby—something to fit in as time allowed. Recent retirement afforded her the luxury of spending gobs of time working on stories that she had been aching to tell. She lives in southwestern Pennsylvania where she and her husband, Ray, raised a daughter and son and where she continues to keep the memory of Chester, their black lab, close to her heart.

www.ingramcontent.com/pod-product-compliance
Lightning Source LLC
Chambersburg PA
CBHW022146170626
46807CB00005B/2102